The Twelve Epic Sagas in the Ancient Chronicles

of the

Sacred Realms

By: Benjamin Quito, PhD.

Book 1: The Dawn of Realms: Origins and Cataclysm

Before the Sacred Realms were shaped, before mountains pierced the heavens and oceans sang their endless hymns, there was only the Eternal—unseen, unchanging, the breath and source of all that would come to be. From His voice, stars ignited like scattered jewels, and the Vastmere Expanse stretched forth beneath the gaze of the celestial sentinels. What began in radiant light soon birthed lands, skies, and seas, each woven with purpose, each declaring the majesty of their Maker. Yet within this grandeur, a singular creation was formed from dust and breath—beings fashioned in His likeness, entrusted with stewardship, intimacy, and choice.

But choice, as the chronicles reveal, is both gift and peril. What unfolds in this *First Stage* is a saga of brilliance marred by shadow—a journey from cosmic beauty to terrestrial tragedy. Mankind, though crowned with honor, falters beneath the weight of temptation. Brother's blood stains the earth, hearts grow corrupt, and what was once good must be cleansed for the sake of redemption's unfolding. Yet through judgment, a thread of mercy weaves quietly, anchoring the promise that darkness shall not reign unchecked.

These are not mere tales—they are the foundations upon which the Sacred Realms stand. Five cataclysmic events shape this era, each echoing through ages to come: the birth of creation, the fall into shadow, the clash of brothers, the flood of judgment, and the sundering of tongues. Through them, the Eternal's justice and mercy intertwine, setting the stage for a covenant that will arise from a single man whose faith will alter the destiny of nations.

Chapter 1

The Celestial Weave

The Shaping of the Veiled Expanse.

In the primordial hush, when silence reigned as the sole sovereign and the void stretched infinite and fathomless, there came forth a moment beyond reckoning—a moment when the Eternal One, whose essence transcends thought and tongue, uttered the first decree.

In the beginning...

A whisper reverberated through the nothingness, a soundless breath that bore creation itself. From the abyssal depths of nonexistence, reality unfurled like a tapestry drawn from the folds of eternity. It was neither an explosion of chaos nor a fleeting spark but a purposeful act—an unveiling of realms yet to be known, yet to be seen.

Thus emerged the vast heavens, an endless firmament adorned with unseen potential, stretching beyond mortal comprehension.

Beneath this newly formed expanse, the earth took form—at first, a formless void shrouded in a mantle of darkness, cloaked in swirling mists and waters untamed. The breath of the Eternal hovered above the deep, a presence unseen yet omnipotent, brooding over the waters like a sentinel awaiting the dawn of purpose.

It was in this sacred stillness that the Eternal One's voice resounded—not with the cacophony of mortal tongues but with a resonance that carved through the void, ancient and immutable. It was a command, a proclamation woven with absolute authority and infinite care.

"Let there be..."

And so, with that utterance, the unfathomable chasm of darkness trembled. The fabric of nothingness was torn asunder, and the first light was born—radiant, pure, unmarred by shadow. It did not merely illuminate; it revealed, exposing the chaos and cloaking it in the warmth of divine purpose. This was no ordinary glow but the very essence of illumination, a beacon that pierced the eternal gloom.

The Eternal beheld this newborn radiance and deemed it good—perfect in its brilliance. He then separated the light from the dark, drawing a boundary between what would be day and what would be night. Thus, was established the cycle—the eternal dance of light and shadow, the rhythmic pulse upon which all realms would find their measure.

And so concluded the first breath of creation: the dawn of time, the awakening of existence. From the nothingness emerged purpose, and from the darkness, a flicker of hope—the herald of wonders yet to be wrought by the hands of the Eternal.

The heavens stretched in silent witness, and the earth, though yet untamed, awaited the shaping touch of its Maker. A story had begun, one that would echo through the ages of the Sacred Realms—etched in stone, whispered in winds, and remembered in the hearts of all creation.

The First Dawn – The Kindling of Light.

In the beginning, the realms were naught but an endless expanse of shadow, a formless void where darkness coiled and stretched without end. Silence reigned supreme until the Eternal One, whose voice transcends the fabric of existence, uttered a single decree that rippled through the nothingness:

"Let there be Light."

In an instant, darkness was cleaved asunder. Light, pure and radiant, burst forth like a river of molten gold, flooding the void and unveiling what had never been seen. It did not simply illuminate; it revealed the raw expanse of potential, the canvas upon which all things would be wrought. Shadows recoiled to the edges, banished yet lingering.

The Eternal separated the light from the darkness, bestowing upon them names: Day for the brilliance, Night for the shadowed repose. Thus, was born the cycle—the endless dance of light and dark, the heartbeat upon which time itself would pulse.

And the Eternal beheld the light, and it was good. So ended the first dawn, as the new realms breathed their first sigh beneath the divided heavens.

The Second Dawn – The Forging of the Firmament.

Once more, the voice of the Eternal One echoed through the nascent expanse:

"Let there be a vault to divide the waters."

The primeval waters, vast and untamed, churned in response. From their swirling depths, a mighty expanse emerged—a shimmering firmament stretched like a radiant canopy across the realms. Waters above were lifted to the high heavens, while those below pooled into deep, glistening seas.

The firmament gleamed with iridescent hues, a celestial veil upon which clouds would one day gather and storms would dance. This vault, broad and unfathomable, cradled the realms beneath it, dividing what was above from what lay below. And the Eternal named this expanse the Heavens.

He beheld His work, and it was good. Thus waned the second dawn, with the skies stretched vast, awaiting the mysteries to come.

The Third Dawn – The Emergence of Land and Verdure.

Then the Eternal spoke with a voice that made the depths shudder:

"Let the waters under the heavens be gathered into one place, and let dry land appear."

In obedience, the waters recoiled, swirling into vast, glittering seas. From their retreating waves rose the land—jagged peaks clawed toward the heavens, valleys yawned with cavernous depths, and plains stretched out like sleeping giants. The Eternal named the dry ground Earth, and the gathered waters, Seas.

But the land was barren, empty of color and life. The Eternal, with words woven in purpose, called forth abundance:

"Let the earth sprout vegetation."

At once, the soil heaved and split. Tender shoots erupted, carpeting the ground in emerald waves. Grasses unfurled, caressing the newborn breezes. Trees stretched their limbs skyward, their branches adorned with leaves that glistened like green fire. Blossoms bloomed in dazzling arrays of color, filling the air with the first fragrances of life. Vines coiled in intricate patterns, and forests swayed in silent reverence.

The Eternal gazed upon the vibrant earth, alive with verdure and promise, and it was good. The third dawn closed with the land clothed in nature's first song, awaiting the luminaries to mark its days.

The Fourth Dawn – The Illuminaries of the Heavens.

Then came the Eternal's voice again, rolling across the expanse like a tide of thunder and wind:

"Let there be lights in the heavens to separate day from night, to mark times, seasons, and years."

The firmament quivered, and from its depths, two great lights emerged. The first blazed with fierce golden fire, casting warmth and brilliance across the lands—a beacon to rule the day. The second, softer and silver-hued, rose to reign over the night, bathing the earth in gentle luminescence.

But the heavens did not rest with just two. Countless lesser lights ignited across the celestial canvas, twinkling like scattered jewels upon a velvet tapestry. Stars, vast and innumerable, flickered with quiet wisdom, their light carrying whispers of ages yet to unfold. They wheeled and spun in silent dance, weaving patterns that would guide, inspire, and mystify.

The Eternal beheld the dazzling heavens, now crowned with radiant watchmen, and it was good. Thus, the fourth dawn waned, leaving the skies ablaze with eternal lights and the earth basking in their cycles.

The Fifth Dawn – The Birth of Creatures of Sky and Sea.

Again, the Eternal's voice surged through the realms, stirring the seas and skies alike:

"Let the waters teem with living creatures, and let birds soar across the expanse of the heavens."

The oceans heaved with joyous tumult as life erupted from their depths. Leviathans, immense and serpentine, glided through the waters with scales gleaming like onyx and sapphire. Great beasts with finned tails and luminous eyes navigated the abyss, their movements stirring the seas into frothing waves. Shoals of radiant fish darted beneath the surface like living jewels, while strange, wondrous creatures of myriad forms swam in depths unseen.

Above, the skies awakened. Wings stretched and unfurled, cutting through the air with newfound grace. Vast birds with feathers shimmering like burnished metal soared across the firmament. Smaller creatures flitted between the branches of newly formed trees, their songs filling the air with the first notes of melody. Winged beasts of majesty and wonder glided on high winds, tracing patterns against the heavens.

The Eternal blessed them, saying, *"Be fruitful and multiply, fill the waters of the seas, and let the skies be filled with flight."*

And so, the waters roared with life, and the skies danced with wings, each creature moving to the rhythm of creation's grand song. The Eternal beheld this symphony of movement and sound, and it was good.

Thus passed the fifth dawn, the realms alive with breath, motion, and the beauty of living forms.

The Sixth Dawn – The Emergence of Beasts of the Land.

With dawn's light glimmering upon earth and sea, the Eternal spoke once more:

"Let the land bring forth living creatures according to their kind."

The earth rumbled and heaved as creatures burst forth from its soil. Mighty beasts with iron-like horns charged across the plains, shaking the ground with their thunderous steps. Sleek hunters with eyes like molten amber prowled through forests, their muscles rippling beneath coats of fur and scale. Herds of massive creatures, their hides like living stone, grazed in the open fields, their calls echoing like distant drums.

Tiny creatures, swift and agile, darted through grasses; burrowing things tunneled beneath the soil. In the forests, beasts with gleaming eyes observed from shadows, while serpent-like creatures slithered with quiet menace across the earth.

Each kind found its place: some to roam the high crags, others to dwell in shadowed woods or sunlit meadows. The land pulsed with newfound life, a chorus of growls, chirps, roars, and whispers filling the air.

The Eternal beheld the land teeming with creatures, each formed with purpose, each flourishing in its domain—and it was good.

Thus closed the sixth dawn, the realms adorned with sky-born fliers, sea-dwellers of wonder, and earth-bound beasts. Life, in all its wildness and beauty, spread across the lands, awaiting the culmination of the Eternal's grand design.

The Crafting of Flesh and Soul.

The six great dawns had passed. The heavens shone resplendent with celestial fires, the lands teemed with beasts both mighty and meek, the seas churned with life, and the skies danced with winged splendor. Yet amidst this abundance, there remained a longing—a vacancy in the grand design. The creatures roamed, the winds whispered through the forests, and the rivers sang to the stones, but none among them bore the mark of consciousness that could mirror the Eternal's thought, perceive His wonders, or share in His creation's purpose.

And so, upon the sacred ground of Elyndor—the cradle of first life—the Eternal One descended in radiant majesty. His presence stirred the winds, and the trees bowed in silent reverence. The earth itself quivered, sensing the imminence of a work unlike any other wrought upon its surface.

He descended. The Lord of all existence, whose breath had summoned stars and whose voice had carved mountains, now reached into the soil He had formed. His hands, immeasurable in power yet tender with an artisan's care, gathered the dust of the earth—fine grains kissed by the winds of the heavens and moistened by the dew of the early realms. This was no ordinary dust; it was the essence of the land itself, the clay of creation infused with purpose.

With deliberate grace, He shaped it. Fingers traced the lines of form: a broad brow to ponder mysteries, hands fashioned to mold and wield, feet to tread the expanse of the realms. Muscles coiled beneath sculpted flesh; veins formed conduits for life's coming surge. Eyes— closed for now—were carved with care, destined to behold wonders and weep sorrows. The figure lay still, perfect in form yet lifeless, like a masterful statue awaiting its animating spark.

Then, the Eternal One leaned close. The vastness of the heavens seemed to hold its breath. His face neared the clay visage, and from His lips flowed the *Breath of Life*—not mere air, but a living essence, a divine ember that transcended flesh. It poured forth as a luminous mist, entering the nostrils of the lifeless form.

For a heartbeat, stillness reigned.

Then—the chest heaved. Air rushed into lungs for the first time. Eyes fluttered open, revealing depths of awareness and light. Fingers flexed; limbs stirred. The man sat up, blinking at the brilliance of the heavens above, his gaze reflecting the spark of his Maker. He inhaled deeply, the scents of earth and sky filling his senses. No longer mere clay, he was now a living soul—bearing the likeness of the Eternal, a bridge between the realms and the divine.

The Eternal beheld him with satisfaction, yet the work was not yet complete. Though life now coursed through the man's veins, a shadow of solitude touched his heart. The creatures had their kind— flocks in multitudes, beasts in herds—but the man stood alone. And it was not good.

Thus, the Eternal caused a deep slumber to descend upon the man, whose eyes closed in peaceful surrender. As he slept, the Eternal reached to his side, where flesh and bone intertwined with divine design. From that place, He drew forth a portion—bone yet not bone, flesh yet not flesh—malleable in His sovereign hands.

With delicate yet resolute craftsmanship, the Eternal shaped this new form. Her frame was fashioned with equal care yet imbued with grace distinct from the man—strong yet soft, elegant as the flowing rivers and fierce as the storm winds. Her hair, like woven strands of night sky, cascaded down her shoulders; her eyes, when they would open, would mirror the depths of the seas and the spark of the stars. Where the man bore the strength of earth, she carried the rhythm of life's nurture and the melody of companionship.

When His work was done, He breathed upon her as He had done before, and warmth spread through her form. Lashes quivered; her lips parted for her first breath. Slowly, she opened her eyes—luminescent and filled with the same divine spark. She arose, standing beneath the canopy of heavens that seemed to gleam brighter at her awakening.

The Eternal brought her to the man. His slumber lifted, and as his gaze beheld her, wonder overtook him. She was no beast of the field nor creature of the skies but flesh of his flesh, bone of his bone—a reflection of himself and yet gloriously distinct. In her eyes, he saw companionship, in her smile, the promise of unity.

The Eternal's work was complete. Man and woman stood beneath the vast heavens, the final jewels of creation's crown—equal in worth, harmonious in purpose. The trees swayed in celebration, rivers murmured hymns of joy, and the stars above kindled brighter flames in witness.

And the Eternal beheld them both, and it was very good.

The Seventh Dawn – The Silence of Completion.

The six mighty dawns had come and passed. The heavens shimmered with radiant luminaries, the seas roared with abundant life, the skies danced with winged creatures, and the lands teemed with beasts and verdure. Man and woman stood upon the earth, the final flourish of the Eternal's masterwork. Creation, vast and intricate, pulsed with newfound life and order—a symphony complete.

Then, as the seventh dawn rose, no command echoed forth from the Eternal. No new form emerged from dust; no waters churned at His voice. Instead, an encompassing stillness descended upon the Sacred Realms. The winds softened, carrying whispers instead of gales. The rivers, which once raced with youthful vigor, now meandered in gentle reverence. Even the stars seemed to hold their twinkling breath.

For on this day—the Seventh Dawn—the Eternal One ceased from His labor. Not from weariness, for what hand could tire that formed the cosmos? No, His rest was not of exhaustion but of divine fulfillment, a sovereign cessation to behold and savor the grandeur of all He had wrought.

He ascended to the heights beyond the heavens, where mortal gaze could never reach and even the stars dared not intrude. There, upon the unseen throne above thrones, He gazed upon His creation—a masterpiece vast and immeasurable. Light danced with shadow in harmonious rhythm, seas glistened like molten silver beneath the golden sun, and the lands stretched wide in splendor. Creatures stirred in their realms, the man and woman walked in serene wonder, and the skies unfolded in brilliant hues.

And the Eternal reflected. His gaze pierced through every expanse—every blade of grass, every drop of water, every heartbeat of life—seeing that it was not merely good, but perfectly complete. A symphony whose final note lingered in sacred stillness.

In this divine pause, the realms themselves seemed to breathe in unity. Mountains stood as sentinels in solemn tribute, forests bowed their branches in quiet worship, and the vast seas stilled their restless waves in reverence of the Creator's rest. It was as though all existence joined in the sacred silence, a cosmic hush honoring the One who had spoken all into being.

And upon this Seventh Dawn, the Eternal sanctified the day. He imbued it with a holiness beyond mortal comprehension—a day set apart, not for labor or toil, but for reflection, gratitude, and reverence. This divine rest established an eternal pattern, a rhythm woven into the fabric of time itself: six dawns for work and wonder, one for peace and reflection.

Thus, the Seventh Dawn passed not with clamor or creation but with profound quiet—a silence that spoke louder than any word uttered before. It was the silence of completion, the peace of perfection. The realms, now whole, basked in the Eternal's blessing, forever marked by the day when the Maker rested, and the world exhaled in harmony.

Chapter 2

The Lament of Shadows

The Fall of Man.

The Sacred Realms, clothed in splendor and harmony, thrived under the gaze of the Eternal. The man and the woman, fashioned by divine hands, walked in the serenity of Elyndor's Haven—the garden forged at the heart of the world. There, rivers of crystal flowed through meadows adorned with blossoms that sang at dawn's light, and trees stretched toward the heavens, their branches heavy with fruits that gleamed like jeweled offerings.

Elyndor was a place untouched by sorrow, where the breath of the Eternal lingered in the air, and all creation moved to a rhythm of peace. The man and woman, clothed in innocence, knew not shame nor shadow. They spoke with the Eternal in the cool breath of the mornings, their hearts unburdened by fear. In this sacred place, every dawn was a promise of unbroken fellowship.

Yet beyond the veiled edges of the garden, darkness stirred. Not in the trees nor in the rivers, but in the unseen corners where pride and ancient rebellion slithered unseen. It was in this hidden place that the shadows found their voice.

The narrative of innocence was about to unravel.

The Boundaries of Trust.

In the heart of Elyndor's Haven—where rivers gleamed like molten glass and trees bore fruit that shimmered with hues unseen beyond the garden's veil—stood two ancient sentinels. These trees, unparalleled in majesty and significance, reached their branches toward the heavens as if to touch the face of the Eternal. One was the Tree of Everlasting Life, whose leaves whispered songs of eternal peace. The other, its twin in stature but contrasting in destiny, was the Tree of the Knowledge of Good and Evil. Its fruit glistened like precious gems under the sun's gaze, radiant yet ominously inviting.

It was before these trees that the Eternal One brought the man—crafted from the dust, imbued with divine breath, and crowned with stewardship over the Sacred Realms. The air pulsed with a sanctified stillness as the Eternal's presence, luminous and beyond mortal sight, enveloped the garden. His voice, when it came, resonated with both warmth and unwavering authority—a voice that had summoned stars into being and stilled the tumult of the primordial seas.

"Of every tree in this garden, you may freely partake," the Eternal spoke, His words flowing like a river—gentle, yet deep with weight. The man's gaze drifted across the verdant abundance surrounding him: orchards heavy with fruits, vines thick with berries, and blossoms exhaling fragrant delight. Freedom was his to savor, abundance his to embrace.

But then the Eternal's voice shifted—still tender but now edged with solemnity. The air seemed to grow heavier, and even the trees bowed their branches in reverence to what was spoken next.

"But of the Tree of the Knowledge of Good and Evil," the Eternal declared, *"you shall not eat."*

The words lingered, echoing through the garden's expanse. The man's gaze settled upon the forbidden tree—its fruit glistening like drops of amber fire, alluring yet untouched. There was beauty in it, but a beauty veiled in danger, as a flame's glow is beautiful yet consumes what dares to embrace it.

"For in the day that you partake of it," the Eternal's voice deepened, carrying the gravity of eternal truth, *"you shall surely die."*

Death. A word foreign to the man's ears—alien in a world unmarred by sorrow. Yet the weight of it pressed upon his soul, stirring a primal understanding: to cross this boundary was to sever the harmony that enveloped him. The command was clear, the boundary drawn not from cruelty but from a Father's wisdom—an invitation to trust, to obey, to dwell within the safety of divine counsel.

The garden, vibrant with life, seemed to hush in the aftermath of the command. Birds ceased their songs; the rivers, though still flowing, whispered more gently. Even the winds, which moments before danced playfully through the leaves, now carried the weight of sacred caution.

The man stood in contemplation; the choice etched into the fabric of his existence. Obedience was not a chain but a shield; disobedience, though cloaked in seeming freedom, bore a hidden blade. The Eternal's gaze—though unseen—rested upon him with both fierce love and unwavering justice.

Thus was the boundary set: a line drawn between trust and rebellion, life and death. The garden awaited. The realms held their breath. The man's journey had begun—cradled between the promise of everlasting communion and the peril of a single choice.

The Whisper of Shadows.

Elyndor's Haven basked in a tranquil glow, where rivers sang soft melodies, and the trees swayed under the golden embrace of the sun. The man and the woman moved through the garden in harmony, their hearts unburdened, their souls intertwined with the Eternal's presence. Innocence cloaked them like a radiant garment, and in that innocence, they found joy beyond mortal comprehension.

Yet not all beings gazed upon the beauty of creation with reverence. Beyond the haven's veiled edges, where the shadows thickened and the light waned, another presence stirred—ancient, cunning, and twisted by pride's venom. It was one who had once basked in the Eternal's light but now seethed with envy, seeking to unravel what he could not destroy. His hatred burned not against creation itself, but against the intimacy shared between the Eternal and His cherished beings.

And so, he came—not with thunder or flame, but with subtlety sharper than any blade. He adorned the form of a serpent, a creature of grace and shimmering scales, its movements fluid like the streams it slithered beside. In those days, the serpent was not yet a symbol of dread but of beauty—elegant, mesmerizing, and wise in appearance. Cloaked in iridescent hues that caught the garden's light, it coiled among the branches of the Tree of the Knowledge of Good and Evil, its body weaving between the boughs heavy with radiant fruit.

The woman, drawn by the tree's allure and the serpent's curious gaze, approached. Her footsteps were light upon the moss-laden ground, her eyes reflecting wonder and a hint of question. The serpent's tongue flickered, tasting the air, before it spoke—its voice soft as velvet, yet laced with a chilling undertone.

"Is it true," the serpent began, its tone feigning innocence, *"that the Eternal has said you shall not eat from any tree in the garden?"*

The woman's brow furrowed, her gaze shifting from the serpent to the fruit that gleamed like molten jewels. *"We may eat the fruit of the trees,"* she answered, *"but of this one, the Eternal has commanded us not to eat or even touch it, lest we perish."*

A smile—if such a creature could possess one—curved upon the serpent's maw. Its eyes, like twin pools of dark fire, fixed upon her with unwavering focus. The air around them seemed to thicken, the garden's vibrant hum quieting as if nature itself held its breath.

"You shall not surely die," the serpent murmured, each word a silken thread weaving doubt into her heart. *"No... the Eternal knows that on the day you partake, your eyes shall be opened. You will not remain as you are. You will ascend—you shall be as gods, knowing good and evil."*

The words hung in the air like forbidden incense—enticing, dangerous, irresistible. The serpent's voice slithered into the crevices of her mind, wrapping around her thoughts like coiling vines. It spoke not only to curiosity but to the hunger for wisdom, the desire for autonomy—to grasp what was withheld, to claim what seemed unjustly denied.

The woman's gaze returned to the fruit. It shone with a captivating glow, promising knowledge, offering empowerment beyond her current understanding. Could the Eternal truly wish to keep such enlightenment from them? Was this command a boundary of protection—or of restriction? Her heart pounded with conflicting waves of loyalty and longing.

The serpent watched with patient satisfaction. It had planted the seed; now desire did its silent work. The allure was not just the fruit—it was the promise that she could shape her own destiny, stand apart from dependence, and wield knowledge meant only for the divine.

In that moment, the haven's gentle breeze seemed to fade, replaced by a suffocating stillness. The rivers ceased their singing; the leaves ceased their dance. All of Elyndor's Haven—no, all of the Sacred Realms—stood on the precipice, awaiting her choice.

Temptation had spoken. Shadows pressed close. And the realms held their breath.

The Shattered Covenant.

The garden of Elyndor stood bathed in ethereal light, where every leaf gleamed as though kissed by stardust, and the rivers mirrored the heavens in perfect clarity. Yet beneath the canopy of the Tree of the Knowledge of Good and Evil, that light seemed to waver. A subtle darkness clung to the air, unseen but palpable, like a gathering storm hidden behind a painted sky.

The woman stood before the tree, her breath shallow, her gaze fixed upon the forbidden fruit. The serpent's words echoed in her mind, a haunting refrain that refused to be silenced: *"You shall be as gods… knowing good and evil."* Her eyes traced the fruit's surface—it glistened with dew, its skin like polished amber flecked with molten gold. It was beautiful. It was alluring. Every sense urged her closer.

"Is it truly forbidden?" The thought slithered through her consciousness. The Eternal had spoken… yet here was the serpent's promise—a tantalizing alternative, a door to wisdom and power beyond her current understanding. Her heart warred within her chest: one beat for loyalty, another for longing.

Her fingers reached out—hesitant, trembling—then pulled back. A breath hitched in her throat. The garden around her seemed to blur, the vibrant colors dulling beneath the weight of indecision. She glanced at the man beside her, his gaze uncertain yet unwaveringly upon her. Neither spoke. Words were unnecessary; the battle raged in silence.

Her gaze returned to the fruit. *"It is good for food…"* Hunger stirred, though not merely of the flesh. *"It is pleasant to the eyes…"* Beauty, irresistible and enchanting. *"And desirable to make one wise…"* Wisdom—knowledge—autonomy.

Her hand moved again, slower this time, drawn as if by an unseen force. Fingertips brushed the fruit's smooth surface, sending a shiver down her spine. Still, the heavens remained silent; the earth did not quake. Could the serpent's words be true?

Her resolve broke. Fingers tightened. The fruit twisted free from its branch with a soft snap—a sound small, yet it reverberated through the realms like a distant bell tolling. She cradled it, heart pounding, the serpent's gaze burning into her from the shadows.

Then—she bit.

The flesh of the fruit was sweet, yet as it slid down her throat, a strange bitterness bloomed. Warmth surged through her body, followed by an unsettling chill that coiled around her heart. Her eyes widened as a flood of awareness rushed in, drowning innocence beneath waves of knowledge too vast, too heavy. The world around her shifted—colors sharpened, shadows deepened, and with clarity came a piercing sense of vulnerability.

She turned to the man, eyes glistening with both wonder and dread, and offered him the fruit. No words passed between them; none were needed. His gaze flickered between her face and the fruit—the choice was his to make. His jaw tightened. And yet... he took it.

He raised it to his lips. The moment stretched, a heartbeat suspended between obedience and defiance. Then he, too, bit.

Silence.

And then—

The air thickened. A cold wind whispered through the trees, carrying with it an unfamiliar weight. Their hearts raced. Their gaze shifted to themselves, and for the first time, they saw—truly saw—their own nakedness. Shame, foreign and sharp, pierced them like a blade. What had been pure was now profaned; what had been peaceful now churned with turmoil.

They tore leaves from nearby branches, hastily weaving crude coverings to hide their exposed forms. Yet no garment could conceal the ache that gnawed at their souls—the unbearable realization of what they had done.

Elyndor's Haven, once a sanctuary of joy and light, now felt alien. The trees seemed to loom with judgment; the rivers, once their song, now whispered accusations. Above them, the heavens watched in solemn silence.

They had seen.

They had desired.

They had taken.

And the Sacred Realms would never be the same.

The Covenant of Dawn.

Before judgment fell with its full weight, before the final severing of man and woman from the sanctuary of Elyndor's Haven, the Eternal, in His boundless mercy, spoke words that would echo through the eons. These were not words of immediate comfort, nor were they easily understood by the ones who heard them. Yet woven within the fabric of His judgment was a thread of hope—a glimmer of light piercing the darkness that had fallen upon creation.

Turning His gaze toward the serpent—the vessel of deception, the harbinger of ruin—the Eternal One proclaimed a decree that would shape the fate of the Sacred Realms:

"I will place enmity between you and the woman, and between your seed and her Seed; He shall crush your head, and you shall bruise His heel."

These words were more than a sentence upon the deceiver—they were a prophecy, a promise, a covenant of redemption. In that moment, the Eternal did not merely pronounce judgment; He unveiled the first glimmer of a grand and redemptive plan. Though the serpent had struck, corrupting what was pure and severing the harmony of creation, its triumph was destined to be fleeting.

This declaration—known through the ages as the *Protoevangelium*, the *First Gospel*—was the spark of a redemptive flame that would blaze through the chronicles of time. It foretold the coming of a Redeemer, born of the woman's lineage, who would confront the darkness that had wormed its way into the heart of the world. The battle would be fierce, and though the Redeemer would bear the scars of this cosmic conflict—His heel bruised by the serpent's strike—the final blow would belong to Him. Evil's head would be crushed beneath His heel, its power shattered beyond repair.

The gravity of this moment cannot be overstated. Where there should have been only wrath, there was mercy. Where there should have been utter despair, there was the seed of hope. To the man and woman, still reeling from the weight of their transgression, the full meaning was obscured, like a distant star barely visible through a stormy sky. Yet the Eternal's words planted something indelible in the soul of creation—a certainty that this brokenness was not the final chapter.

Throughout the unfolding of the Sacred Realms, this promise would be the guiding light for those who clung to faith. Prophets would arise, speaking echoes of this covenant. Kings would rule and fall with hearts yearning for its fulfillment. Priests would offer sacrifices that pointed forward to the ultimate sacrifice yet to come. Every shadowed valley and every glimmer of light in the chronicles ahead would trace its roots back to this singular promise.

And the serpent—though it slithered away into the darkness—carried the weight of that decree. It knew that its seeming victory was tainted with inevitable defeat. No scheme, no deception, no force of darkness could unweave the words the Eternal had spoken.

For the promise of the Redeemer was not merely a hope—it was an unbreakable decree. In the fullness of time, the Seed would come, wielding truth like a blade and bearing the weight of redemption upon His shoulders. He would suffer, yes, but He would conquer. His heel would bleed, but the serpent's head would be crushed.

Thus, from the ashes of rebellion, the Covenant of Dawn was forged—a promise that would echo through every realm, every age, every heart that longed for restoration. The darkness had made its move. But the Eternal had spoken. And when the Eternal speaks, His words do not return empty.

Hope was born. Redemption was set into motion. And the Sacred Realms, though marred by shadow, would never be without the light of that promise.

Chapter 3

The Brothers of Blood and Shadow

Sin, once a distant shadow cast beyond the gates of Elyndor's Haven, had now crept into the fabric of mortal existence. What began as a whisper in the garden—a small act of disobedience—had festered, deepening its roots within the hearts of humankind. Like a slow-moving poison, it seeped from thought to action, from fleeting envy to irreversible consequence. The ground itself, which once bloomed with purity under the gaze of the Eternal, now bore witness to the weight of that darkness.

The tale of Drevak and Thalen, the firstborn sons of the fallen pair, stands as the Sacred Realms' earliest testimony to the far-reaching tendrils of sin. Born into a world both breathtaking and broken, the brothers could not escape the inheritance of their parents' choice. They were raised amidst remnants of paradise and the bitterness of exile, their lives shaped by the tension between light remembered and shadow encroaching.

Drevak, the elder, toiled upon the earth—an earth that resisted his every effort, its soil grudging beneath his hands. His labor was harsh, his heart heavy with the burden of proving himself worthy. Thalen, the younger, tended flocks that grazed upon the wild meadows, his spirit attuned to the whispers of the wind and the soft pulse of life beneath his feet. Two brothers. Two paths. Yet beneath the surface of their daily toil stirred unseen forces: pride, jealousy, devotion, and longing.

But this is no mere tale of rivalry; it is a chronicle of the heart's descent when untended desires fester. Envy, when left unchecked, breeds darkness far deeper than anger. And when pride demands what is not freely given, the soul stands at a precipice—one step away from ruin.

In this tale, offerings are made, hearts are laid bare before the Eternal, and choices are forged in the furnace of emotion. It is here that devotion meets rejection, and anger kindles flames that cannot be extinguished. Blood will be spilled upon the earth—blood that cries out beyond the veil of the living, echoing into the very heavens.

This is the story of Drevak and Thalen. Of blood and shadow. Of choices made and consequences borne. It is a somber reminder that the greatest battles are often not waged with blade and shield, but within the chambers of the heart—where darkness whispers, and the choice to listen shapes the destiny of realms.

Flames of Devotion and Pride.

The winds of the Sacred Realms carried with them the scent of earth and ash as dawn unfurled its golden tendrils across the horizon. In this new world—beautiful yet marred by the echo of ancient disobedience—human hearts wrestled with unseen burdens. Though the Eternal's voice no longer walked openly among them, His presence lingered in the breath of the wind, the pulse of the rivers, and the stirrings of the conscience. Deep within their souls, the children of the fallen pair understood that reverence must be offered to the Eternal One, for life itself was a gift requiring acknowledgment.

Drevak and Thalen, born of the same blood yet bearing hearts as different as night and dawn, prepared their offerings. The reasons behind their acts—whether born of a quiet command from the Eternal or an innate awareness of their fractured state—remained a mystery lost to the winds of time. Yet what is known is this: both approached the altar, yet not with the same heart.

Drevak, whose hands bore the calluses of countless days tilling unyielding soil, gazed upon the fruits of his labor. His fields had fought him—thorns clawing at his arms, the earth resisting every seed he planted—but through sweat and stubbornness, he had forced it to yield. He gathered produce from the land: grains hard-won, roots torn from the reluctant earth, and fruits that gleamed beneath a thin sheen of dust. These, he reasoned, should suffice. To Drevak, his offering was proof of his toil, a testament to his endurance and effort.

Thalen, meanwhile, moved among his flocks beneath the pale glow of the morning sky. His sheep stirred around him, soft bleats breaking the predawn silence. He knelt beside a ewe and gently lifted a lamb—a firstborn, flawless and unblemished. Thalen's gaze lingered on the creature, his heart heavy with reverence and sorrow. The sacrifice was not given out of obligation but out of gratitude, a recognition of the

Eternal's provision amid a world shadowed by loss. With careful hands, he prepared not just any lamb but the choicest of the firstborn, ensuring the fat portions—the richest and most valued parts—were included. His offering was not a token of effort but an outpouring of worship.

The brothers ascended to the place of offering—a stone altar weathered by the elements, standing like a silent sentinel between earth and sky. Flames crackled to life as each presented his gift. Drevak laid his produce upon the stones, the colors of fruits and grains vibrant in the flickering light. His jaw tightened as he stepped back, arms crossed, eyes glancing at his brother. Thalen approached in turn, laying the lamb's remains upon the fire, the aroma rising with a richness that mingled with the smoke, ascending into the heavens like a whispered prayer.

The air grew still. Time seemed to stretch, every heartbeat echoing in the silence that followed. Two offerings. Two hearts laid bare. The Eternal, unseen yet ever-present, beheld both. Acceptance and rejection were soon to be revealed, but it was not the outward gift that weighed most heavily—it was the spirit in which it was given.

Drevak's gaze shifted between the rising smoke and Thalen's bowed form. Pride and uncertainty warred within him. Thalen stood with calm humility, unaware—or perhaps unconcerned—with how his brother's eyes darkened with something that flickered between doubt and simmering resentment.

In this moment, choices were made not just with hands, but with hearts. And the Sacred Realms, witnesses to this solemn rite, braced for what would come next.

The Shadowed Heart.

The flames from the altar still smoldered, their smoke curling into the vast skies as the unseen gaze of the Eternal judged what lay before Him—not just the offerings but the hearts from which they sprang. The air thickened with an unseen weight. Drevak's offering, though laid with hands hardened by toil, was rejected. Thalen's, given in humility and reverence, was received with favor. In that revelation, something within Drevak fractured.

A fire ignited—not the holy flames upon the altar, but a darker inferno burning in his chest. His heartbeat quickened, pounding with a fury that seemed to reverberate through his very bones. His breath grew ragged, hands clenched into fists so tight his knuckles whitened. How could this be? Had he not toiled? Had he not fought the stubborn earth to wrest forth its yield? Yet the Eternal had turned from his fruits and smiled upon Thalen's offering. Thalen—the younger, the shepherd whose hands bore no scars of plowing fields, whose face wore that insufferable calm.

Jealousy seeped like poison into Drevak's veins. His gaze found his brother, who knelt in quiet gratitude beside his accepted offering. That serenity was salt in a festering wound. *Why him?* The question roared within Drevak's mind, louder with every heartbeat. *Why not me?* His vision clouded, the world blurring into shades of red and shadow. Pride twisted into bitterness. Bitterness into hatred.

Thalen approached, eyes gentle, voice soft. "Brother—" The single word was an offering of peace, a bridge across the growing chasm. But to Drevak, it was a spark to dry tinder.

"Do not call me that!" Drevak's voice erupted, venom-laced and jagged. His glare could have carved stone. Thalen recoiled, sorrow dawning in his eyes. Yet pity only fueled the fire.

Dark whispers, born of envy and pride, coiled through Drevak's thoughts. *He stands in the light that should be yours. He steals the favor meant for you. Remove him, and the shadow will lift...* The voice was not his own, yet it echoed with dreadful clarity within his mind.

Reason faltered, consumed by the storm within. Rage clouded conscience. And so, Drevak, heart twisted beyond recognition, spoke words that dripped with false warmth: "Come, brother. Let us walk to the fields beyond the rise."

Thalen, ever trusting, nodded and followed. His footsteps were light upon the earth, while Drevak's pressed deep, as if the ground itself recoiled from him. The meadow stretched before them, golden grasses swaying beneath the gentle breath of the wind. But nature's beauty was lost on Drevak, his gaze fixed on a single, dark purpose.

They reached a solitary glade, hidden from sight. Thalen turned, a question forming—but it never found voice. Drevak's hands moved with grim finality. There was no hesitation. No mercy.

The act was swift. Terrible. Final.

Blood spilled upon the earth, staining the soil that had once refused to yield for Drevak. The ground drank deeply of the crimson flow. Thalen's eyes— once vibrant with life—dimmed, his final breath a whisper lost to the wind. His blood seeped into the earth, a silent cry echoing beyond mortal ears to the heavens themselves.

Drevak stood over the lifeless form, chest heaving. The fury ebbed, replaced not with triumph but with a yawning abyss. Silence surrounded him—but it was the kind of silence that crushed, that deafened with guilt. He looked at his bloodstained hands—trembling now—and a hollow realization clawed at him: he had slain his own brother.

Sin, once a shadow, had now fully revealed its monstrous form. The darkness within Drevak had not merely taken hold; it had devoured. And yet, beyond that glade, the Sacred Realms seemed to hold their breath. The earth had received blood unjustly shed—and it would not remain silent.

This was more than brother slaying brother. It was the unveiling of how deeply sin could root itself in the human soul—how unchecked envy could birth hatred, and how hatred, left to fester, could drive one to spill the blood of his own kin.

And even in that blood-soaked silence, the need for redemption screamed louder than ever. The Covenant of Dawn—whispered after the first fall—now glowed brighter against the darkness unfolding. For if the earth cried out at Thalen's blood, how much louder would the cry for a Redeemer become?

The Curse of the Wanderer.

The glade lay silent, save for the faint rustling of leaves stirred by a mournful wind. Blood darkened the soil, and the earth—ancient witness to countless dawns—had opened to receive what should never have been shed. Drevak, standing over his brother's lifeless form, felt the weight of the act press down upon him like an iron shroud. His hands, stained crimson, trembled not from exhaustion but from the dawning realization of what he had done. His chest heaved, lungs desperate for breath, as if air itself recoiled from him.

And then—the voice of the Eternal broke the silence.

It did not thunder as a storm nor blaze like consuming fire; no, it came with a stillness more terrifying than any fury, penetrating bone and soul alike.

"Where is Thalen, your brother?" The question was not asked from ignorance, but to unearth the depths of Drevak's heart.

Drevak's lips parted, a feeble attempt to hide the truth—but what deception could veil itself before the All-Seeing? *"I... I do not know,"* he lied, words tasting like ash. *"Am I my brother's keeper?"*

The wind seemed to halt; even nature recoiled at the brazen falsehood. Then came the Eternal's response—a declaration not merely heard, but felt through marrow and spirit:

"What have you done? The voice of your brother's blood cries out to Me from the ground."

Drevak's knees buckled beneath the weight of those words, his heart pounding with dread. No earthly judgment could match the gravity of what followed.

"And now... you are cursed from the earth, which has opened its mouth to receive your brother's blood from your hand."

The words fell upon him like an avalanche, unrelenting and absolute. The very soil beneath his feet seemed to pulse with rejection, pushing him away. Where once the earth begrudgingly yielded to his toil, now it would refuse him entirely. Fields would wither under his touch, and no harvest would grow in soil marred by fratricide. His labor would be in vain—his every attempt at stability swallowed by futility.

But worse still was the final pronouncement, echoing like an eternal tolling bell:

"A restless wanderer you shall be upon the face of the earth."

Wanderer. Exile. A soul without anchor, forever adrift. The weight of the curse settled upon Drevak, heavier than any chain forged by mortal hands. He would walk the realms with no place to rest his head, haunted by the absence of the brother whose life he had stolen. Every landscape would turn foreign, every horizon a reminder of what he had lost—and what he had become.

His mind raced with memories: Thalen's laughter, their shared childhood under the canopy of Elyndor, fleeting moments of brotherhood now twisted into torment. The blood on his hands was not just his brother's—it was a stain that seeped into his very soul, impossible to cleanse.

The Sacred Realms seemed to hold their breath as the curse hung in the air, final and irrevocable. There was no pleading that could undo it, no penance that could erase the crime. Sin, born of envy and pride, had reached its full bloom, and the harvest was ruin.

Drevak stood, hollowed and broken. The wind resumed, whispering through the trees, carrying with it the echo of Thalen's blood and the silent cries of the earth. He turned from the glade—eyes shadowed, steps heavy—and began to walk. Each footfall a journey into exile. Each breath a reminder that, though he lived, he carried within him a death far worse than the grave.

The curse was not just upon his flesh—but upon his very name, a mark that would follow him across the ages. And so, the first murderer of the Sacred Realms became its first wanderer, his path stretching endlessly before him—a road paved with regret, shadowed by guilt, and haunted by the inescapable weight of justice.

The Seed of Renewal.

The Sacred Realms, though darkened by the stain of Drevak's crime, did not remain without a glimmer of hope. Judgment had fallen, blood had soaked the earth, and shadow had stretched across the land— but the Eternal, rich in mercy, was not yet done with His creation.

Adam and Elyria, burdened by sorrow too deep for words, grieved for their lost sons—one slain, the other exiled. The weight of loss pressed heavily upon them, their days shadowed by regret and longing. Yet amid the ashes of tragedy, the Eternal bestowed a gift—a promise that darkness would not have the final word.

In the passing of seasons, Elyria conceived again, and to them was born another son—a child whose cry pierced the stillness like a dawn breaking through endless night. They named him **Sethariel**, meaning "appointed"—for he was given to take the place of Thalen, whose blood still cried out from the earth. The child's eyes shone with a quiet light, his presence a balm to wounds that time could not wholly mend.

As Sethariel grew, so too did the remembrance of the Eternal among the people. In his days, hearts once silenced by fear and sorrow began to stir with reverence anew. Voices, long muted, rose in song and supplication, calling upon the name of the Eternal with renewed fervor. Beneath star-lit skies and beside ancient trees, altars were raised—not in the pride of works nor in the shadow of envy, but in humble devotion and longing for restoration.

And so, through Sethariel, the righteous lineage continued—an unbroken thread woven through time, a line that would carry the promise of redemption whispered since the fall. Though shadows still prowled, and darkness waited at every turn, the light of that promise—faint yet unwavering—flickered on.

The Sacred Realms turned their gaze toward the horizon, where future sagas awaited, born of sorrow yet gilded with hope. For even in the aftermath of blood and shadow, the Eternal's hand moved still, guiding hearts toward the dawn that would one day break with radiant finality.

Thus ends the tale of **The Brothers of Blood and Shadow**—a tale of envy and grace, of ruin and renewal. But the chronicles are far from over. For as long as the earth endures and the stars bear witness, the story of redemption marches onward, carried by the seed of promise and the lineage appointed for salvation.

Chapter 4

The Deluge of Shadows and Reckoning

The Sacred Realms, once vibrant with the breath of creation, had grown heavy with corruption. Generations had risen and fallen since the days of Drevak and Thalen, yet as time unfurled its relentless march, the hearts of mortals darkened further. Violence roamed unchecked, echoing across the lands and waters; pride and wickedness flourished where once reverence had dwelled. The earth itself, groaning beneath the weight of bloodshed and unbridled depravity, seemed to mourn for what had been lost. Shadows that began with a single act of disobedience now covered the world like an encroaching storm.

Why must the first world face destruction? How had corruption seeped so deeply into every corner of creation that it warranted such sweeping judgment? These questions loom as ancient voices whisper from the dust and rivers carry the weight of forgotten sorrows. Yet amid the darkness, there remained one family—one lineage through which the Eternal's covenant of hope would be preserved. A righteous man named Vaelen, set apart from the corruption of his age, was chosen as the vessel of survival, through whom the promise of redemption would sail above the waves of ruin.

As the floodwaters prepare to rise, deeper questions swirl within the chronicles of the Sacred Realms: From where did the multitude of nations and races spring forth, each bearing its own customs, tongues, and lands? How did the scattered peoples trace their lineage back to those who survived the cataclysm? And in the unfolding saga, what destiny awaited the descendants of Vaelen's sons? From whose bloodline would arise the patriarch whose journey would reshape the fate of realms? Whence came the separation of the kindred—Zareon and Lothar—whose paths would diverge, setting into motion stories of promise, conflict, and divine providence?

These mysteries, woven through the tapestry of the Sacred Realms, await unraveling as the heavens prepare to open and the earth to break. For in the face of impending destruction lies the seed of restoration, and in the judgment of the first world, the foundation is laid for the rise of nations and the forging of destinies yet to be fulfilled.

The storm gathers. The skies darken. And the chronicles turn to one of the most harrowing and hopeful sagas of all—the great deluge that would cleanse the world of shadow and pave the way for the promise to endure.

The Reckoning Foretold.

The Sacred Realms, once illuminated by the Eternal's breath of life, had descended into a mire of corruption and darkness. Generations of men, birthed from the seed of the fallen, walked the earth not with gratitude, but with greed, not with reverence, but with rebellion. Violence coursed through the veins of nations, deceit dripped from tongues like venom, and every heart seemed a wellspring of wickedness. What had begun as a spark of disobedience in the garden had now become a wildfire, consuming the very fabric of mortal existence.

The Eternal, whose gaze pierces the soul and sees the shadow behind every smile, beheld the realms—and sorrow gripped His heart. He had breathed life into dust, had sculpted beauty from nothingness, yet what stood before Him was a creation twisted by pride and corruption. Every thought, every intention born within the hearts of humankind, spiraled into darkness without end. There was no rest from evil, no pause in the clamor of wickedness.

And so, with grief immeasurable and justice unwavering, the Eternal's voice thundered through the heavens and across the lands:

"Behold, the wickedness of man is great upon the earth. Every imagination, every thought of his heart is set upon evil, continually and without cease. My spirit shall not strive with mortals forever. I am grieved to My core. Therefore, I shall cleanse the earth, wiping man from its face—the beast of the field, the bird of the skies, and the creeping things shall fall with him. For I regret what has become of what I once declared good."

The words rippled through the realms, carried by winds that howled through forests and stirred the deepest seas. Mountains trembled, rivers recoiled, and the stars seemed to flicker in mourning. Nature itself shuddered beneath the weight of impending judgment.

But this was no impulsive wrath—it was a decree born from patience long-suffering and mercy long-offered yet spurned. The Eternal's grief was not that of regret in creation, but sorrow over what creation had become. His justice, like an ancient blade unsheathed, would strike not out of malice, but necessity. For corruption, when left unchecked, spreads until nothing pure remains.

A warning had been spoken. A reckoning had been declared. The Sacred Realms stood upon the precipice of annihilation. Yet even in the shadow of destruction, a faint ember of hope flickered—for the Eternal, in His justice, had not forgotten mercy.

But the floodwaters waited. The skies darkened. And mankind, blind to the coming storm, danced on the edge of oblivion.

Vaelen Found Favor.

Amidst the storm of corruption and the darkness that engulfed the Sacred Realms, there flickered a single, steadfast light. While the hearts of mortals waxed cold and the lands were soaked in violence,

there was one man whose soul had not been swallowed by shadow—
one whose steps echoed with reverence and whose heart, beat in rhythm
with the will of the Eternal.

Vaelen.

He was a man set apart, a solitary figure standing against a
world cascading toward ruin. While others schemed and stained the
earth with blood, Vaelen walked a different path—one paved with
integrity, humility, and unwavering faith. His eyes beheld the same
darkness that consumed his generation, yet he did not yield to its allure.
The corruption that ensnared others found no hold upon him, for his
heart was a sanctuary where the whispers of the Eternal found
welcome.

The Eternal beheld the Sacred Realms, marred and twisted
beyond recognition, and His gaze settled upon Vaelen. In a world
where wickedness reigned supreme, here stood a man who sought
righteousness. A man who, though surrounded by deceit, spoke truth,
who, though encircled by evil, acted justly. Vaelen was not sinless, yet
his repentance was genuine, and his devotion unshaken.

And so it was that amidst declarations of judgment and the foretelling of destruction, the Eternal's voice softened with mercy:

"But Vaelen has found favor in My eyes."

Words simple in utterance, yet profound in consequence. In the vast expanse of a world ripe for obliteration, one man—one family—would become the vessel through which life would endure. Through Vaelen's obedience, the spark of humanity would not be extinguished. His name would be remembered not merely for survival, but for faith that stood resilient against the rising tide of darkness.

The days ahead would not be easy. Judgment loomed like a tempest on the horizon, and the weight of an unfathomable task would soon rest upon his shoulders. Yet with favor came purpose, and with purpose, a calling that would test the limits of endurance and trust. Through Vaelen and his household, the earth would be cleansed and, in time, replenished. But this new beginning would come not without cost, for they would bear witness to the sweeping hand of justice and the echoes of a world drowned in its own iniquity.

Still, amid the gathering storm clouds and the murmurs of coming wrath, one truth remained unshaken: *Vaelen found grace in the eyes of the Eternal.* And through that grace, hope was kindled anew—a fragile ember destined to survive the deluge and light the path for generations yet to come.

The Cataclysm of the Ancient Realms.

The skies brooded with darkening clouds, swirling like an ominous shroud over the Sacred Realms. For years, Vaelen's voice had echoed through cities and wilderness alike, proclaiming warnings that fell upon deaf ears. His words, like thunder before the storm, spoke of justice long withheld and wrath long delayed—but no longer. *"Turn back! Repent!"* he cried to those whose hearts had been calcified by wickedness. Yet mockery answered him. Laughter rang louder than reason, scorn sharper than swords. The people feasted in their corruption, danced in their violence, and reveled beneath skies that darkened with every passing dawn.

And through it all, Vaelen built. Planks were shaped by hands calloused with obedience; timbers joined beneath a sun that seemed to withhold its warmth. The structure rose—a colossal vessel unlike anything the realms had ever beheld—its wooden frame a testament to faith amidst ridicule. The ark stood as both sanctuary and omen: salvation for the few, condemnation for the many. As each beam was laid, it seemed the heavens themselves watched in solemn silence.

Days stretched into years, yet the corruption of humankind only deepened. The ground was soaked in bloodshed, the air heavy with lies and cruelty. Yet amidst this darkness, the Eternal's instructions guided Vaelen's every step. *"Make it long and strong. Make it endure what is to come,"* the Divine had commanded. And so he labored, his sweat mingling with prayers, his breath a constant plea for strength.

Then—the day arrived. The air shifted, thick with an expectancy that set creatures and men alike on edge. The Eternal's voice, like a wind that filled every corner of the realms, spoke to Vaelen with finality: *"Enter the ark—you and all your household. For the appointed hour of reckoning has come."*

And so, Vaelen led his family into the vessel, their footsteps echoing hollowly against the wooden floorboards. But they were not alone. From across the lands, beasts of every kind emerged—summoned by a power beyond mortal comprehension. Lions padded alongside lambs; serpents slithered beside sparrows. Predators and prey moved in harmony, drawn by the Eternal's unseen hand. Wings beat the air as flocks descended, and the ground trembled beneath the march of hooves and claws. The ark's shadow swallowed them one by one until the doors, massive and ancient, creaked shut—sealed not by mortal hand, but by the Eternal Himself.

And then—the skies broke.

A single drop fell, dark and heavy, striking the parched earth with a hiss. Then another. And another. Until rain cascaded from the heavens like silver spears. The clouds churned, vomiting torrents as winds howled like anguished spirits. Lightning tore through the darkness, illuminating faces twisted in horror and disbelief. Rivers swelled with monstrous speed, consuming fields, homes, and temples once thought invincible. Mountains shuddered as the earth itself seemed to convulse in agony.

The mockers, those who had laughed at Vaelen's warnings, now clawed at the rising waters, voices raised in frantic pleas—but it was too late. Waves surged like ravenous beasts, devouring all in their path. Trees snapped like brittle twigs; mighty walls of stone crumbled beneath the weight of the flood. The Sacred Realms dissolved into an endless expanse of churning, merciless waters.

Inside the ark, darkness reigned but for the flickering glow of lanterns. The rhythmic pounding of rain against wood was an unyielding reminder of the chaos beyond. Vaelen knelt with his family, heart heavy with both sorrow and gratitude—sorrow for those lost to their defiance, gratitude for the favor that had spared them. Above and around them, the wrath of the Eternal swept over the world in relentless waves.

The first world had been given every chance. Warnings had been spoken. Patience had been extended. Yet sin had refused to release its grip. And so, judgment fell—not as a cruel whim but as the necessary cleansing of a world too far gone.

The floodwaters rose until no mountain peak breached their surface. The realms that once bustled with life now lay silent beneath a vast, unforgiving sea. Death reigned upon the surface, but within the ark—a remnant, a promise, and the seed of a future yet to be written endured.

For though judgment had come like a tempest, the Eternal's covenant lingered like a hidden ember beneath the waves—waiting, watching, ready to spark anew when the waters would at last recede.

The Birth of Realms and Peoples.

The floodwaters, once a wrathful sea that consumed the realms, began to ebb. Day by day, the relentless waves receded, revealing a world cleansed of its former corruption—yet marked by the scars of judgment. Where once cities and forests stood, there now stretched barren plains and jagged rocks. The silence that followed was deafening, broken only by the cries of distant wind and the slow drip of water from fractured cliffs. It was a world reborn, awaiting new breath, new footsteps, and new life.

Within the ark—weathered by storm and time—Vaelen and his family emerged beneath the open sky. The air was fresh with the scent of rain-soaked earth and new beginnings. Their eyes scanned the horizon, hearts heavy with the weight of all that had been lost, yet stirred by the promise of what could now rise. The Eternal's voice, both thunderous and tender, reached them with clarity beyond sound:

"Behold, I bless you. Be fruitful. Multiply. Fill the earth and replenish what has been lost."

And so began the next great chapter of the Sacred Realms—the seeding of nations from the remnants of a single family. Vaelen's sons—Seryn, Halvar, and Jareth—each bore within them the spark of future peoples and kingdoms. Their descendants would stretch across the lands, carving out realms, languages, and traditions that would one day stand at odds, ally in peace, or clash in war. The rivers would bear their ships, the mountains their fortresses, and the fields their harvests. What had been empty would soon teem with life anew.

Seryn's lineage would become known for wisdom and reverence, birthing scholars, priests, and rulers whose influence would shape the spiritual heart of the realms. Halvar's bloodline, fierce and unyielding, would spread across the southern lands—nations of warriors and builders, resilient against both nature and foe. Jareth's descendants, wanderers at first, would traverse seas and forests, founding kingdoms along distant shores, their culture diverse, their tongues many.

From these three branches would arise the multitude of peoples: some seeking the Eternal's guidance, others turning to shadowed paths, but all tracing their origins to the family that stepped off the ark into the dawning light. Nations would rise with pride, histories would be forged in stone and song, and across the ages, the names of Seryn, Halvar, and Jareth would echo through both time and legend.

Yet with this blessing came responsibility. The earth had been cleansed once by water, a reminder etched into the mountains and valleys that wickedness would not be tolerated without consequence. The new peoples would carry this history—a tale of mercy mingled with judgment—guiding some toward righteousness, and others into rebellion.

The Sacred Realms expanded, life unfurling like a tapestry woven from threads of promise, trial, and choice. The Eternal's command to fill the earth was not merely about multiplying in number, but about stewarding what had been renewed. Each nation born from Vaelen's sons would face that choice: to honor the Covenant of Dawn—or to walk the paths of those whose voices were drowned beneath the ancient waves.

Thus, the origin of nations was not just a beginning—it was a test. A trial that would unfold across generations, with destinies intertwined and futures shaped by the choices of many yet unborn.

Chapter 5

The Shattered Tongues of Caldreth

The Sacred Realms, though cleansed by floodwaters and renewed under the gaze of the Eternal, once more bore witness to the relentless corruption of the human heart. Time had passed since Vaelen's sons had filled the lands with descendants, and where humility should have taken root, pride grew in its place. Prosperity bred arrogance; unity, once a gift, became a weapon wielded against the very One who had spared them from annihilation.

As generations flourished, so too did ambition, twisting hearts toward rebellion. The memory of the flood—of a world drowned in consequence—faded like a shadow at noon, replaced by a dangerous confidence in human ingenuity. With one tongue and one voice, the people conspired not to honor the Eternal, but to exalt themselves, reaching toward heights not meant for mortal grasp. What was born of cooperation became an edifice of defiance, and the skies—once symbols of promise—became their target for conquest.

This is not merely a tale of a tower rising from the plains of Caldreth; it is the revelation of mankind's relentless pursuit to dethrone the Eternal, to claim glory not theirs to wield. Like the stories of Drevak's envy and Vaelen's generation's downfall, this account underscores the futility of a heart severed from reverence. Pride blinds. Ambition without humility destroys.

And so, as stones stacked upon stones and voices chanted in unified rebellion, the heavens prepared to respond. The Eternal—patient beyond comprehension—would act not with flood, but with confusion. Words, once bridges between souls, would become barriers. Unity would fracture. Nations would splinter.

For when mankind dares to ascend beyond their ordained place, the very foundation beneath their feet is destined to crumble.

Thus begins the saga of the **Shattered Tongues of Caldreth**—a testament to the folly of pride and a reminder that no kingdom built on defiance can stand against the will of the Eternal.

The Ascension of Pride.

The Sacred Realms, vast and varied, stretched out with mountains cloaked in mist, rivers that glistened like silver veins, and valleys ripe for settlement. The Eternal's command had been clear: *"Spread across the lands, fill the earth, and steward what has been given."* Yet, the hearts of men, ever drawn toward defiance, saw not a world to cherish but an opportunity to consolidate power.

Led by ambition and united by a single tongue, the descendants of Vaelen gathered upon the plains of Shinar—a land where fertile ground met open skies. Here, they devised a plan that would defy both heaven and destiny: *"Let us build for ourselves a city, and within it, a tower whose peak shall pierce the very heavens!"* It was not shelter they sought, nor community for safety—it was renown, immortality through monument. A structure that would challenge the very dominion of the Eternal.

Laborers toiled under the sun, their bodies drenched with sweat, driven not by necessity but by the intoxicating promise of glory. Kilns burned day and night, forging bricks from clay that darkened like hardened blood. Pitch flowed like rivers of shadow, binding stones together into an edifice that clawed at the clouds. The tower rose, defiant and unyielding—a spine of arrogance stretching into the sky.

Men stood upon its ascending levels and gazed downward, pride swelling in their chests. *"Look upon our work!"* they proclaimed. *"No flood shall scatter us again. No judgment shall find us here! We shall be as gods, our name eternal!"* Songs of ambition echoed between the scaffolding, chants resounding as bricks ascended higher. Children were told tales of the tower's inevitable ascent to the stars, and elders spoke of a future where none could surpass their dominion.

But beneath their fervor lay the root of rebellion: a refusal to heed the Eternal's design. Unity, once a gift to foster compassion and growth, had been twisted into a weapon of defiance. Instead of spreading across the realms to cultivate and cherish the earth, they sought consolidation—to make themselves untouchable, invincible.

The tower was not just stone and mortar; it was a testament to humanity's lust for autonomy—a structure born of pride, fear, and an insatiable hunger for significance apart from the Eternal. And while the city's streets bustled with life, and the tower's shadow stretched far over the plains, the heavens watched in silent judgment.

For even the tallest towers built by mortal hands crumble when their foundations rest upon arrogance.

The Confusion of Tongues.

The tower of Caldreth clawed at the heavens, its shadow stretching long across the plains. Day after day, laborers toiled under the blazing sun and chill moonlight, their voices echoing with chants of ambition and pride. Hammers rang against stone, and furnaces blazed as bricks were forged and raised ever higher. The air was thick with dust, sweat, and the intoxicating fervor of a people united in defiance. *"We shall ascend! We shall make our name eternal!"* they proclaimed, the tower standing as a spine of rebellion against the heavens.

But above their lofty ambitions, beyond the veils of cloud and sky, the Eternal beheld their work—and His gaze did not waver. He saw not only the structure rising from the earth but the hearts behind each stone placed. Pride had fermented into arrogance. Unity, once a divine gift, had become a tool to exalt man above their Creator. Their tongues, one and the same, had become a weapon wielded against the very One who had breathed life into them.

And so, the heavens stirred. The Eternal's voice, ancient and immeasurable, reverberated through the celestial realms: *"Behold, they are one people, and they all share one tongue. Nothing they plan will be withheld from them. Let Us descend, and there— confuse their language, that they may not understand one another's speech."*

What followed was not a tempest nor a blaze of celestial fire— but something far more unsettling. As dawn broke over Caldreth, workers gathered as they had for countless mornings. Commands were shouted—but the words, once clear, fell upon ears that could no longer comprehend. A mason called for stone, but the bearer stared back, confused. A foreman barked orders, but his crew responded with foreign syllables, alien and dissonant. Laughter turned to bewilderment. Frustration gave way to panic.

Conversations that once flowed like rivers became fractured streams of noise and chaos. Tongues twisted, familiar words crumbling into incoherent fragments. Friends gestured wildly, hands grasping for meaning that slipped through their fingers like mist. Shouts of confusion echoed through the scaffolding, growing louder than the hammers and tools now abandoned. What had begun as unity unraveled before their eyes—a tapestry of language torn asunder by invisible hands.

Some tried to adapt, miming their intentions with frantic gestures, but what could not be spoken could not be built. The tower's ascent ground to a halt. Bricks remained unmoved, tools lay scattered, and scaffolds creaked under the weight of abandoned ambitions. Anger flared as misunderstandings bred conflict. Alliances dissolved, friendships crumbled, and chaos reigned where once there had been order.

It was not destruction by flood or fire—but something far more lasting. Words—the very means by which hearts and minds connect—

had become a barrier, a chasm impossible to cross. Pride had united

them in rebellion; confusion now scattered them in defeat.

Realizing their efforts were futile, groups began to break away

from the plains of Caldreth. Each clan, drawn together by the fragments

of their new tongues, drifted in separate directions. Some ventured into

the mountains, others into forests and far-off valleys. What had been

one people was now a multitude of tribes, nations in their infancy,

speaking tongues that would echo through the ages as reminders of this

day.

And so, the city was abandoned. The tower, half-finished, stood

like a monument to human arrogance—a spine of stone piercing the sky

but forever incomplete. Wind howled through its hollow chambers, and

vines would soon creep along its weathered stones, nature reclaiming

what pride had tried to elevate.

Above it all, the heavens remained silent, the Eternal's

judgment delivered. There was no need for further wrath. The

confusion of tongues had undone the ambition of men more thoroughly

than any sword or storm could. And as the peoples scattered across the

Sacred Realms, their voices—once unified—became a cacophony that would echo for generations to come.

Thus, the folly of pride was laid bare, and the chronicles of the Sacred Realms turned their page from rebellion to dispersal. No tower of man, no matter how high, could ever reach beyond the dominion of the Eternal.

The Sundering of Nations.

The city of Caldreth, once alive with the clamor of ambition and the chorus of unified voices, now stood eerily silent. The confusion of tongues had fractured what was once a seamless unity. Workers, artisans, and leaders who once communicated with ease now stared at one another with bewildered eyes, their words like foreign music clashing against ears that could no longer comprehend. Friendships dissolved into frustration, partnerships into discord, and what had been a grand vision now lay in ruins, its incomplete tower clawing at the sky like a broken finger pointing in accusation.

The Eternal's judgment was clear. Pride had driven men to ascend beyond their place, and confusion had severed the thread that bound them. Yet, the consequence did not end with mere misunderstanding—it was dispersion. In the days that followed the unraveling of speech, people began to gather in groups, drawn together by the fragments of language they could still understand. Confusion turned to necessity, and necessity to migration.

From the plains of Caldreth, they departed. The once bustling city emptied, its grand ambitions abandoned. Dust gathered on the stones, and the towering monument, now a hollowed relic, became a warning to generations yet to come.

Those who spoke with a tongue clear to their own ears ventured eastward, their paths winding through vast stretches of wilderness and sweeping plains. These were the descendants of **Seryn**, the eldest of Vaelen's sons, whose people carried a sense of purpose rooted in tradition and reverence. They crossed rivers that shimmered beneath the gaze of distant stars, climbed ridges where winds sang through ancient trees, and at last settled in the lands that would one day stretch across the heart of the Sacred Realms—a region destined for wisdom, poetry, and the fostering of deep spiritual heritage.

Others, whose speech had splintered into rougher, earthier tongues, journeyed southward. They were the children of **Halvar**, rugged and strong, their spirits undaunted by the sun-scorched deserts and tangled jungles they encountered. These travelers pressed into lands where the air thickened with heat and the earth was rich with minerals and life. They built their homes along great rivers and in the shadow of towering mountains, forming societies that would thrive on endurance, craftsmanship, and a fierce resilience against the harshness of nature.

To the west, the descendants of **Jareth** set their course. Their journey took them through dense forests and over rolling hills, beyond mist-laden valleys where the ground was soft with moss and the skies often wept with rain. These people, diverse in temperament, spread across vast territories—some settling near the coastlines, others forging deeper into unknown lands. Their settlements became hubs of trade and exploration, cultures rich with song, seafaring, and the restless pursuit of new horizons.

The scattering was not immediate nor without hardship. Families were torn apart; bonds severed by the simple inability to speak or understand. Yet, driven by survival and the need for belonging, the scattered peoples found new homelands. Nations began to rise from the footprints of their wanderings, and as seasons turned to generations, the memory of Caldreth's tower faded into legend—a cautionary tale passed down in differing tongues, each version a distorted reflection of the truth.

Above it all, the Eternal watched. His decree had not been born of cruelty, but of divine wisdom. Had they remained united in rebellion, their corruption would have deepened beyond repair. Scattering was mercy as much as it was judgment, a dispersal that would eventually seed the Sacred Realms with cultures and peoples diverse and wondrous.

And so, the descendants of Vaelen spread across the face of the earth. Their languages evolved, their customs diverged, and the lands they inhabited bore the marks of their unique journeys. Mountains, rivers, forests, and deserts—all would echo with the voices of these scattered peoples, each tongue a reminder of both mankind's pride and the Eternal's sovereignty.

Though they would forget the cause of their dispersal, though kingdoms would rise and fall, and wars ignite between those who once shared a single tongue, one truth would remain unaltered through the ages: No ambition, no tower, no kingdom forged from human pride could ever ascend beyond the reach of the Eternal's will.

The Lineage of Seryn: The Chosen Bloodline.

Amidst the scattering of nations and the rising tapestry of tongues and tribes, one lineage stood marked by the Eternal's hidden hand—a bloodline preserved through the ages, not for wealth or conquest, but for destiny beyond mortal comprehension. From the sons of Vaelen, **Seryn**, the eldest, bore the mantle of promise. His descendants, though scattered among the eastern lands, carried within their veins a covenant unseen, yet unbreakable. Their journey through generations would weave a thread of hope through the darkness of the Sacred Realms.

The scrolls of ancient lore, etched in the tongues of the elders and guarded by the keepers of knowledge, recount the lineage born of Seryn's seed. Names passed down like whispered prayers, each life a step toward a future unseen but sovereignly ordained:

From **Seryn** was born **Arveth**, whose years stretched long, witnessing the rise of fledgling kingdoms and the fading memories of the flood's cataclysm. Arveth's wisdom, though quiet, shaped his kin to walk humbly, their steps echoing with reverence toward the Eternal's ways.

Arveth begot **Lerak**, whose hands tilled the earth and whose voice sang laments for a world increasingly consumed by ambition. In Lerak's days, cities flourished with pride, yet his family remained set apart—pilgrims in lands that welcomed their labor but not their devotion.

Lerak's lineage continued through **Dalen**, a man of unwavering resolve, whose gaze seemed to pierce beyond the present into realms of promise unseen. To Dalen was born **Ebron**, whose name carried the weight of endurance, for his days were shadowed by growing corruption among the surrounding peoples.

Ebron's son, **Selvar**, journeyed far from ancestral lands, seeking places where the Eternal's name was not yet forgotten. He fathered **Mareth**, whose heart burned with longing for purpose beyond the fleeting ambitions of mortal kings.

Mareth begot **Ezir**, and from Ezir came **Teresh**, a man whose household grew amidst lands of strife, yet whose lineage remained untainted by the lust for dominion that gripped other nations. Teresh's son, **Lureth**, passed on the stories of old—the floodwaters that cleansed, the tower that fell, and the promise that endured.

From Lureth came **Nahorim**, whose years were marked by patient waiting, his eyes always lifting toward the distant stars, remembering the tales that one day, through their blood, the realms would know redemption. **Serugath**, his son, walked in similar faith, raising his family in lands where idol altars burned but never bowed his knee to false gods.

Serugath begot **Ebronis**, whose life, though quiet in deeds, bore the promise closer to fulfillment. Ebronis's son, **Tarven**, known among his people as one whose counsel was sought and whose words carried weight, fathered **Zareon**—the man through whom destiny's door would open wide.

Thus, from the loins of Seryn to the birth of Zareon, generations rose and fell like waves upon the Vastmere Expanse. Empires emerged and crumbled, languages shifted like desert sands, and the Sacred Realms marched on through cycles of darkness and fleeting light. Yet through it all, the Eternal's covenant thread remained unbroken— woven through humble lives, through men who walked not in the halls of power but in quiet reverence.

Zareon, the culmination of this chosen line, would bear a calling that stretched beyond mortal comprehension—one that would alter the course of nations, ignite the embers of ancient promises, and set the Sacred Realms on a path toward redemption long awaited.

The lineage of Seryn was more than ancestry; it was prophecy made flesh. And as the chronicles turned their page to Zareon's journey, the heavens themselves seemed to hold their breath—for what was whispered in ages past now stirred to awaken.

Zareon's Forebears – The House of Tarven.

Amidst the sprawling lands of Eldoria, where the rivers gleamed like molten silver and the plains stretched vast beneath starlit skies, there stood the ancient city of **Ur-Valdreth**—a place known for its towering ziggurats, bustling marketplaces, and temples adorned with idols forged from gold and obsidian. Its streets echoed with chants to lesser gods, and incense smoke coiled into the heavens, seeking favor from deities whose silence was as deep as the void. Yet, amid the noise of idolatry and the grandeur of human achievement, there lived a family through whom the Eternal's promise would take root and flourish.

From the honored line of **Seryn**, passed down through generations, was born **Tarven**, a man of somber gaze and contemplative spirit. Though his city thrived with wealth and revelry, Tarven's heart often wandered beyond the walls of Ur-Valdreth, drawn to the stories of old—the ancient flood, the shattered tongues at

Caldreth, and the covenant whispered across his lineage. He held fast to the fading traditions of his forefathers, guarding the spark of truth that many had let flicker out amid the shadows of idolatry.

Tarven's household grew to include three sons: **Zareon**, **Nahareth**, and **Haranis**—each shaped by the weight of heritage yet marked by differing paths.

Zareon, the eldest, bore the quiet strength of his father but with eyes that seemed to pierce the horizon, ever searching for what lay beyond the known. His demeanor was steadfast, his words measured, and though surrounded by a people lost to superstition, his heart remained restless—yearning for a truth untouched by the hands of man.

Nahareth, quick of tongue and sharp of wit, chose to dwell within the comforts of the city's commerce and traditions. He embraced the wealth and influence that Ur-Valdreth offered, finding prosperity among merchants and favor in the courts of local rulers.

Haranis, the youngest, was known for his gentle spirit and compassionate heart. Though he shared Zareon's unease with the city's idolatry, his affections remained close to home, nurturing his family and tending to the needs of his kin. Haranis's son, **Lothar**, was a boy of bright eyes and boundless curiosity, often seen trailing behind his uncle Zareon, absorbing tales of ancient days and distant lands.

Ur-Valdreth, for all its splendor, was a city adrift from the Eternal's ways—its people devoted to stone-carved gods and sky-bound constellations. Temples dominated the skyline, and rituals to appease the deities of harvest, war, and wealth filled the calendars. Yet, within Tarven's household, the old stories lingered in whispered recollections beside the hearth—tales of Vaelen's faith, Seryn's legacy, and a promise that one day, through their bloodline, a greater purpose would unfold.

Despite this glimmer of ancestral memory, darkness pressed ever closer. Haranis's life was cut short by illness, leaving Lothar fatherless but under the protective gaze of his grandfather Tarven and his uncle Zareon. The loss carved a shadow across the family, deepening Zareon's inner turmoil and sense of urgency.

The Sacred Realms churned with shifting allegiances and the rise of kingdoms, but amid this vast tapestry, the Eternal's gaze rested upon one man—Zareon. He, whose footsteps traced the streets of Ur-Valdreth, would soon be called to journey beyond the comfort of hearth and kin, beyond the familiar idols and the flickering fires of his people's fading reverence.

The chronicles thus pivot toward this house of ancient blood, from which would rise not a mere wanderer but a patriarch—a man whose obedience would ignite the unfolding of the Eternal's covenant and reshape the destiny of nations. For in the household of Tarven, amid grief and lingering faith, the stage was set. The call was near. And the journey, both perilous and wondrous, was about to begin.

Epilogue – The Dawn of Covenant and Destiny.

The Sacred Realms, from their inception to the present age chronicled in these ancient tales, have been a tapestry woven with threads of splendor and shadow, of promise and rebellion. Across the expanse of time—through the forging of the cosmos, the shaping of mortal kind, the descent into temptation, and the relentless tide of sin— the Eternal's hand has never withdrawn. His justice has been fierce, His patience unfathomable, His mercy ever glimmering beneath the storm clouds of judgment.

We have journeyed through the *First Stage* of these chronicles, where creation sang with celestial harmony only to be silenced by disobedience's bitter echo. Elyndor's Haven, once radiant with purity, was lost to mankind's grasping hand. Drevak's fratricide stained the earth with brother's blood, and the floodwaters of Vaelen's time cleansed a world that refused repentance. Even after the deluge's receding waves and the rebirth of peoples, the hearts of men swelled again with pride, erecting a tower that sought to pierce the heavens—

and the Eternal, seeing their defiance, sundered their tongues and

scattered their ambitions across the lands.

Throughout these sagas, a singular truth has resounded:

humanity, left to its own devices, spirals into ruin. The darkness is not

merely around them—but within them. Generations rose and fell,

kingdoms flourished and crumbled, and though the Sacred Realms

teemed with life and grandeur, they groaned under the weight of sin's

relentless march. Yet through every judgment, every exile, every

consequence deserved, the Eternal's gaze searched for hearts that would

turn toward Him. For while His justice demands reckoning, His mercy

seeks restoration.

And now, as the chronicles turn their page, the narrative shifts.

No longer will the dealings of the Eternal be broad strokes upon the

canvas of mankind's collective rebellion. The focus narrows—drawn to

one man. One lineage. One covenant that will echo through the ages.

His name: **Zareon**—born of the ancient line of Seryn,

descendant of Vaelen, son of Tarven. A man whose heart, unlike many around him, stirs with questions that the gods of Ur-Valdreth cannot answer. A man who, standing amidst idol altars and fleeting ambitions, senses the hollow ring of mortal pursuits and yearns for a truth beyond carved stone and whispered lies.

The Eternal speaks—not with storms or floods, but with a voice that pierces the soul:

"Zareon, arise. Leave your land. Forsake your father's house. Journey to the land I shall show you. I will make you a great nation. I will bless you, and through you, all the families of the earth shall be blessed."

In this moment, the chronicles pivot. No longer is the story merely of mankind's fall—but of redemption's rise. From Zareon's steps into the unknown shall unfold a saga of covenant, sacrifice, faith, and fulfillment. His journey will birth nations, kings, and prophecies. His lineage will carry a promise older than the stars—that through his seed, a light will pierce the darkness that has long shrouded the Sacred Realms.

This is not merely the end of one tale, but the prologue to a destiny stretching beyond imagination. The Eternal's plan, patient through millennia, now takes form not through floods or tongues scattered, but through a covenant sealed not by human merit but divine grace.

The Sacred Realms stand at the brink of a new dawn. Sin has reigned—but not unchallenged. Darkness has encroached—but not unopposed. For in Zareon's calling, hope kindles anew, and the promise whispers across mountains, rivers, and lands beyond sight:

"Through you... all the families of the earth shall be blessed."

Thus concludes the *First Stage* of *The Twelve Epic Sagas in the Ancient Chronicles of the Sacred Realms*—a foundation of creation, corruption, and the flickering embers of redemption. But the journey is far from over. Ahead lies a path of trials, wonders, and revelations that will shake kingdoms and stir the heavens.

The Eternal has chosen. The saga continues. And the Sacred Realms will never be the same.

Book 2: The Covenant Forged in Shadows and Light

The chronicles now turn from the vast sweep of creation and the descent of mankind into shadow, narrowing their focus upon a singular man and a covenant destined to alter the course of the Sacred Realms. Where once the Eternal's dealings encompassed all peoples, His gaze now centers upon one lineage, one family through whom light shall pierce the darkness, and through whose descendants the nations shall be measured and blessed. This is the *Second Stage*—the saga of patriarchs, promises, and perils—a journey across deserts, kingdoms, and dreams as ancient prophecies unfurl with divine precision.

Within these sagas lies the heartbeat of a covenant forged not in fleeting words but in the crucible of sacrifice, faith, and unwavering obedience. It is a story not merely of men, but of the Eternal's relentless pursuit to redeem a world fractured by pride and sin.

Chapter 1

Zareon and the Path of Covenant

The Path of Forsaken Lands and Promised Horizons.

The sprawling city of **Ur-Valdreth** lay beneath a sky painted in twilight hues, its towering ziggurats catching the dying light like massive fingers clawing at the heavens. Markets bustled with merchants draped in silks from Velithar and Myrren's Port, voices shouting in a cacophony of languages as exotic spices, gleaming jewels, and crafted blades exchanged hands. The streets, paved with black stone, echoed with the clatter of hooves and the calls of criers announcing the latest decrees from the royal court. Temples rose like mountains, adorned with idols forged from precious metals, each one a testament to the people's devotion to gods that demanded sacrifice and promised fleeting favor.

Yet beneath the splendor, Ur-Valdreth pulsed with shadows. Incense smoke curled into the sky, carrying with it prayers to false deities—gods whose stone faces bore cold, indifferent smiles. Rituals drenched in blood and gold unfolded in dim chambers, the cries of supplicants mixing with the laughter of priests drunk on power. Idolatry gripped the city like a serpent coiled around its prey, and immorality seeped into its every crevice. Ur was not just a city; it was an empire—prosperous, vast, and spiritually hollow.

Amidst this world of opulence and corruption walked **Zareon**, son of Tarven. His robes, simple yet well-worn, swayed as he moved through the crowded streets, eyes distant—gazing beyond what was to what could be. His was a soul restless amid wealth, a heart unswayed by Ur's temptations. While others knelt before idols of stone, Zareon found himself drawn to the heavens, to the stars that burned beyond mortal reach. *Was there not more? Was there not One greater?*

It was on a night thick with desert wind and starlight that the call came—silent yet thunderous, a voice that did not speak to ears but to the very marrow of his being:

"Zareon, arise. Leave your land, your kin, and your father's house. Journey to the land I shall reveal. I will make you a great nation. I will bless you, and through you, all the families of the earth shall be blessed."

The words struck him with awe and dread. Leave everything? His homeland, his kindred, the familiar paths of his youth? Yet the weight of the voice carried undeniable authority, laced with promise and purpose beyond mortal comprehension. What was comfort compared to destiny? What was security when weighed against divine calling?

With morning's first light, Zareon gathered his household. His wife, **Sareah**, stood by his side, her gaze steady, her spirit as resilient as the stones beneath their feet. His nephew, **Lothar**, young and full of untested zeal, offered words of encouragement but eyes betrayed questions. Servants and herders joined the caravan, laden with provisions—skins of water, packs of grain, herds of sheep and goats bleating restlessly. With each step away from Ur-Valdreth's gates, the world they knew shrank behind them, swallowed by distance and dust.

The journey northward stretched across leagues of unforgiving desert. The sun blazed like a relentless sentinel, scorching the sands beneath their feet. Nights brought cold winds that howled across the dunes, stirring fearsome shapes that danced in the flickering torchlight. Yet even the harshness of the land paled in comparison to the uncertainty of the road ahead. Raiders lurked beyond rocky outcroppings; serpents slithered beneath the sand. There were days when thirst gnawed at their throats and nights when hunger whispered cruelly.

Weeks bled into months until at last the caravan reached the bustling trade routes along the **Eryndar River**, its waters shimmering like liquid obsidian beneath the moon. This was the path to **Haranis**—a city nestled along the upper reaches of the river, known for its verdant fields and thriving markets. Here, weary bones found brief respite. Lothar marveled at Haranis's towering granaries and bustling harbors; his youthful heart tempted to settle among its comforts. Even Zareon felt the tug—roots sought soil, and Haranis offered stability.

Yet his nights remained restless. Dreams haunted him: visions of stars that danced in patterns unknown, lands unseen, and altars bathed in sacred fire. The voice came again, softer but no less insistent: *"This is not your rest. Arise, Zareon. The journey is not yet complete."*

The death of **Tarven**, his father, weighed heavily upon him during this time—a loss both personal and symbolic. It marked the end of what was and pressed him toward what must be. Mourning passed; purpose prevailed.

And so, after years in Haranis, the caravan once again stirred to life. Through mountain passes where the wind howled like ancient spirits, across plains where wild beasts prowled beneath the tall grasses, they pressed onward. Sareah's endurance became legend among the servants, her steadfast presence a source of strength when doubts crept in. Lothar, now tempered by the journey's rigors, bore scars not just upon his flesh but etched into his character.

At last, the horizon broke into rolling hills and fertile valleys. Streams carved silver veins through the earth, olive groves swayed gently, and wildflowers painted the land in hues unseen for leagues past. They had arrived in the land of **Velithar**, and before them lay

Shekareth, a place cradled between twin hills where ancient oaks

stretched their branches like arms lifted in praise.

It was here, amidst the tranquility of flowing waters and rustling

leaves, that Zareon halted. Dismounting, he knelt upon the earth—rich,

dark soil that promised life and legacy. Stones were gathered—unhewn,

untouched by tool—and an altar rose beneath the open sky. As dusk

unfurled its indigo cloak overhead, Zareon lifted his gaze toward the

myriad stars now glittering like a celestial choir.

"You have called me from my land, O Eternal One," he

whispered, *"and I have come. I know not what lies ahead, but I trust in*

Your voice that summoned me from the dust of certainty into the

wilderness of promise."

A breeze stirred, warm and encompassing, carrying the faintest

of scents—of rain yet to fall, of harvests yet to be sown. It was a

whisper of assurance. Here, in Shekareth, amidst hills that bore witness

to the unfolding of destiny, the first altar was raised, and the first offering given. Not of grain or flesh—but of heart, of surrender, of unwavering trust.

Zareon stood, his face illuminated by the flickering altar flame, and behind him, the Sacred Realms stretched vast and unknown. Before him, the promise awaited. Adventure lay not only in lands to be crossed but in faith to be forged.

The journey had only just begun.

Shadows of Famine and Sands of Fortune.

The skies over **Velithar** darkened with an oppressive pall, clouds heavy with threat yet bereft of rain. The once fertile fields cracked beneath the relentless sun, rivers shriveled into winding scars upon the land, and the olive groves withered as the earth cried out in hunger. Whispers of despair rippled through the people: *"The Eternal's blessing has fled from us."* In the air hung a suffocating stillness—a famine unlike any in living memory.

Zareon stood upon a rocky rise, his cloak billowing in the dry wind, gaze sweeping the barren expanse before him. His herds, once innumerable, now dwindled, gaunt creatures braying in vain for sustenance. Children's laughter had faded, replaced by the hollow echo of empty stomachs and the distant weeping of mothers. Sareah's face, though steadfast, bore lines etched by worry; even **Lothar's** usual zeal dimmed beneath the weight of desperation.

And so, the choice, though heavy, was clear: *survive... or perish.* Southward lay the realm of **Zephyra**—a land of sprawling sands and shimmering cities, where the **Nileth's Vein**, a mighty river, breathed life into the desert's throat. It was said that Zephyra's granaries brimmed with abundance, its rulers wielding power vast as the sea, their palaces gilded with treasures beyond imagining. But the land was also known for treachery cloaked in hospitality and gods as numerous as the stars.

Survival demands risk, Zareon reasoned. With the flick of a hand, he ordered the caravan assembled.

Their journey was a trial by dust and flame. Days blurred into a relentless march beneath a sun that scorched flesh and spirit alike. Nights brought bitter cold, the darkness pierced by wary glances and the flicker of dying campfires. Sandstorms erupted without warning— raging beasts of wind and grit that clawed at their caravan, forcing man and beast alike to seek refuge beneath canvas and prayer.

Yet, as if carved from the sands themselves, the cities of Zephyra emerged—oases of opulence amid desolation. Palm trees swayed in lush courtyards, marble columns gleamed beneath golden banners, and streets bustled with merchants offering silks, spices, and glistening jewels. Zephyra's capital, **Solkaris**, rose like a crown upon the desert, its palace domes shimmering under the sun's relentless gaze.

But with prosperity came peril. Zareon's heart grew troubled upon witnessing how many gazes lingered upon Sareah—her beauty, even veiled, radiant beyond concealment. Zephyra's nobility, known for their appetite for the extraordinary, would not let such splendor pass unnoticed.

And so, fear—raw and urgent—found voice in Zareon's counsel: *"Say that you are my sister,"* he urged Sareah. *"Let this be our shield against their desires, lest they claim you and strike me down."* A choice born of fear; its wisdom dubious—but desperation breeds flawed judgments.

Word of Sareah's beauty spread like wildfire through Solkaris's courts until it reached the ears of the **Pharemon**, sovereign of Zephyra, whose gaze hungered for all that glittered. Envoys, cloaked in finery and armed with honeyed tongues, approached Zareon, offering gifts of livestock, servants, and silver in exchange for her presence at the royal palace. Zareon, torn between dread and necessity, acquiesced—his heart a battlefield of guilt and hope that deception might preserve them.

Within Solkaris's walls, Sareah was draped in garments of flowing silk, adorned with jewels harvested from the depths of the **Obsidian Deep**. Lavish feasts welcomed her, wine flowed like rivers, and melodies filled the air—but beneath the opulence lurked unseen dangers. Sareah's heart, though surrounded by luxury, yearned only for deliverance.

Yet, the Eternal sees beyond façades and hears cries spoken only in the silence of hearts.

Plagues, swift and merciless, descended upon Zephyra's palace. Darkness clouded its halls, and the laughter of courtiers turned to coughing fits and fevered wails. Livestock perished without reason, crops blackened under an unyielding sun, and dreams twisted into nightmares. The Pharemon, shrouded in turmoil, summoned seers and priests, demanding answers—but the gods of Zephyra stood mute.

At last, revelation struck: *"You have taken the wife of a sojourner under false pretenses,"* a seer declared, trembling. *"The wrath upon us is the work of the God he serves—One mightier than all the idols of Zephyra combined."*

Rage and fear entwined, the Pharemon summoned Zareon to his throne. Guards, armed and stern, parted for the sojourner who walked not with pride but with a heart heavy with shame. Before the sovereign, Zareon bowed low, awaiting judgment.

"Why did you deceive me?" the Pharemon's voice thundered, echoing off marble pillars. *"Why say she was your sister, that I might*

take her? Behold how my house suffers for your deceit! Take your wife, take all that is yours, and leave—lest the wrath upon us darken further!"

No further words passed. Driven by urgency, Zareon's caravan was loaded with gifts—flocks swelling in number, servants and camels laden with wealth beyond expectation. Though wealth poured into his hands, Zareon's soul remained burdened by the cost of his choices.

And so, they departed Zephyra's grandeur, traveling northward once more beneath starlit skies. Sareah, seated beside him, laid a hand upon his own—a silent assurance that forgiveness, though hard-earned, was given.

Their return to Velithar was marked by abundance: flocks too vast to count, riches gleaming beneath sunlit banners. Yet Zareon knew that wealth, though plentiful, was not the true reward. Survival had been granted, yes—but so too was a lesson seared into his soul: trust in fear yields folly; trust in the Eternal brings deliverance.

Reaching the lands near **Bethelor**, where hills rolled like slumbering giants and olive trees stretched toward the heavens, Zareon halted once more. Stones were gathered; an altar rose beneath the sky's vast canopy. Flames danced upward, smoke curling heavenward as prayers—of gratitude, of repentance—ascended.

"You have led me through famine and fear, through plenty and peril," Zareon whispered. *"Not by my hand, but by Your mercy, have I returned. Teach me to trust—not in schemes, nor in riches—but in You alone."*

The wind stirred through the trees, rustling leaves like whispered affirmations. In the silence that followed, the Sacred Realms breathed with new purpose. Wealth now adorned Zareon's house, but it was the refining of his heart that marked the journey's true treasure.

Yet, the path of covenant was far from complete. Ahead lay further trials, greater revelations. But for this moment, beneath the Bethelor sky, Zareon stood—a sojourner, a man transformed—his gaze lifted once more to the stars, those ancient witnesses to promises still unfolding.

The Parting of Kindred and Paths.

The Sacred Realms, kissed once more by the favor of rain and fertile winds, blossomed with abundance. Flocks grazed upon the hills, their bleating a song of renewed life; herds trampled the grasses until the earth seemed alive with the pulse of prosperity. Tents stretched across the landscape like scattered sails upon a sea of green, fires flickering as evening shadows danced along the valleys of **Velithar**.

Zareon's camp sprawled across the hill country; tents woven from fine fabrics acquired during the sojourn in **Zephyra**. Silver glinted from trade wares, and his servants' laughter echoed through the camp— yet prosperity, unchecked, often bears the seeds of strife.

Nearby, **Lothar's** encampment stretched vast and restless. His herds rivaled Zareon's, his wealth having swelled from the journey's spoils and the blessings bestowed upon their family. Yet abundance gave rise to friction. The shepherds of both camps quarreled over grazing lands and water rights—arguments that began with harsh words soon escalated to clenched fists and drawn blades. Wells dug by one camp were claimed by the other; flocks, driven together at riverbanks, sparked disputes that echoed across the valleys.

Zareon stood upon a rocky outcrop, gazing down upon the discord brewing like a storm. His brow furrowed, not with anger but with sorrow. *Is this what prosperity has birthed? Have blessings turned brotherhood into bitterness?* He turned toward the tents below, where herdsmen bickered, and servants exchanged venomous glares.

Resolute, Zareon summoned **Lothar** at dawn, when the world was bathed in gold and the morning breeze carried whispers of ancient mountains. His nephew approached; youthful confidence shadowed by the tension that now lay between them. Their journey together had begun with shared hopes and brotherly affection—yet distance had crept in like an unseen fog.

"Lothar," Zareon spoke, voice steady as the stones beneath them, "let there be no strife between us or our herdsmen, for we are kin. This land—vast and generous—need not be the battlefield upon which brotherhood shatters." He turned, arm sweeping across the horizon, where valleys stretched lush, and rivers gleamed like serpents winding through the plains. "Lift your eyes, nephew. Behold the expanse before us. Choose your path—whichever land your heart desires—and I shall journey the other way."

Lothar's gaze followed the gesture. His eyes, bright with ambition, settled upon the fertile plains of **Ardeneth**, where the rivers **Sylora** and **Merith** fed the land like veins coursing with life. Verdant fields rippled with promise, orchards dotted the landscape, and the distant cities shimmered beneath the morning light. Wealth, ease, and power lay that way—a paradise beckoning to one eager for swift gain.

His decision came swiftly. "I shall take the plains," Lothar said, voice tinged with gratitude and hunger for what awaited. "The lands of Ardeneth call to me, uncle—the rivers run full, the fields yield without struggle." He paused, placing a hand upon Zareon's shoulder. "Your kindness will not be forgotten."

Zareon smiled, though a shadow flickered behind his eyes. "Then go with blessing, Lothar. May the Eternal guide your steps."

With farewells exchanged, Lothar's caravan—resplendent with wealth, herds, and servants—snaked down toward the valley, banners fluttering as oxen carts creaked and camels groaned beneath laden packs. Lothar rode at the forefront, eyes fixed on the horizon, dreams of prosperity filling his mind. Beyond those lush fields, however, dark clouds gathered unseen, and the distant cities—though gleaming— harbored shadows that whispered of future sorrows.

Zareon stood upon the hill long after the dust of Lothar's departure settled. He turned from the fertile plains, casting his gaze toward the rugged highlands. The hill country, though less inviting, called to him in ways the valleys never could. Its rocky crags and windswept ridges promised hardship—but also solitude, reflection, and divine communion. There, upon barren heights where few dared dwells, altars could be raised without distraction, and the stars seemed closer, their silent vigil a constant reminder of promises yet to be fulfilled.

Leading his household northward, Zareon's footsteps found purchase upon stony paths. Sareah walked beside him, serenity etched into her features. Servants followed, less enthused by the arduous climb but loyal to their master's course. They passed ancient trees whose roots coiled like serpents through the rock, crossed streams that sang soft songs through moss-laden stones, and finally settled upon a plateau overlooking the lands below.

There, beneath an ancient oak whose branches stretched like arms toward the heavens, Zareon paused. He knelt, gathering stones once more, stacking them in humble reverence. The altar rose—a silent testament to trust beyond sight, to a journey defined not by land's richness but by the Eternal's voice.

Lifting his gaze to the expanse above, Zareon breathed deeply of the crisp, untamed air. The plains glittered afar, but his heart found peace amid the rugged hills. *It is not the land that sustains—it is the promise. And promises forged by the Eternal never fail.*

The wind stirred, rustling the oak's leaves like a whispered affirmation.

The kindred had parted ways, paths diverged. One road led to comfort and allure: the other, to hardship and divine encounter. Yet both roads would bear stories etched into the chronicles of time—tales of fortune, folly, and the ever-unfolding hand of providence.

And so, upon the heights of **Velithar**, Zareon dwelled—rich not in the eyes of men, but in the favor of the Eternal. The plains lay distant, the hills rugged—but his spirit stood unshaken. The journey was far from over. The covenant still whispered. And the stars, ever watchful, burned brighter against the deepening sky.

The Rescue of Lothar – The Midnight Reclamation.

The lands of **Ardeneth**, once a haven of lush fields and glistening rivers, found themselves shadowed beneath the banners of war. Rumors had whispered of an eastern alliance—four powerful kings whose realms spanned beyond the **Obsidian Deep**—rising with ambitions to conquer. Their armies, blackened by countless battles, swept across the lands with relentless purpose, like a storm no walls could halt. Cities that had stood for generations fell under their heel, and none who resisted survived to recount the horrors.

Among their conquests lay the fertile plains of Ardeneth, where **Lothar**—rich in flocks, abundant in gold, yet spiritually adrift—had settled near the decadent city of **Veyloris**. The eastern kings struck swiftly, laying siege to the plains with iron-clad warriors and siege engines that roared like beasts. Fires consumed the land; herds were driven off; tents were torn asunder. Caught unprepared, Lothar's servants fell or fled, and he himself was seized, dragged in chains as a prize of war—his wealth stripped, his dignity trampled.

The invaders, gorged on plunder, marched northward with captives and spoils trailing behind like the tail of a monstrous serpent.

Far in the rugged heights of **Velithar**, word of the calamity reached **Zareon**. When a breathless messenger, dust-covered and trembling, delivered the news of Lothar's captivity, Zareon's heart clenched with grief—and resolve. *Family... forsaken by folly, yet not abandoned.* Blood ties, though stretched by distance and choices, remained unbroken.

"Summon the men," Zareon commanded. His voice, calm yet iron-forged, stirred his camp into urgent motion. Three hundred and eighteen warriors—trained servants, steadfast companions—assembled beneath the twilight sky. They bore no grand armor nor royal standards, but their eyes burned with loyalty, their blades honed not just by metal but by years of shared trials.

As the last embers of day died on the horizon, the force rode out, torches casting flickering shadows upon the rocky paths. Zareon, at the forefront, his cloak billowing behind him, fixed his gaze upon the dark expanse ahead. He was not driven by vengeance—but by a fierce, unyielding duty.

The enemy encampment sprawled across the **Vales of Obryn**, fires illuminating tents bloated with stolen goods. Laughter and drunken revelry echoed through the valley; the conquerors lost in the arrogance of victory. Captives, bound and huddled, bore hollow eyes—among them, Lothar sat, face shadowed with regret, chains biting into his wrists.

Zareon crouched atop a ridge, surveying the enemy. His plan formed swiftly: a divided strike under cover of night—precision over numbers. He turned to his men, voice a low command. "Tonight, we fight not for land nor wealth—but for kin. No mercy for those who show none."

With a silent signal, darkness erupted into chaos. Flames from hastily lit arrows streaked the sky, igniting supply wagons. Warriors descended from all sides like shadow-born phantoms. Blades clashed; cries of shock turned to terror as the revelry shattered into blood-soaked confusion. Zareon cut through the fray, his sword gleaming with every strike, eyes locked on the captive lines.

Lothar's head snapped up amidst the din as Zareon fought his way to him, severing chains with a swift strike. "Stand, nephew," Zareon growled, pulling him to his feet. Lothar, breathless, staggered beside him. "You came..." he managed, voice cracked with disbelief.

"For blood and for bond," Zareon replied, parrying a blade that came too close. Together, they pressed toward the ridge as their men overwhelmed the fragmented enemy. Panic consumed the eastern kings' forces—leaders fled; soldiers scattered. What began as conquest ended in humiliation.

As dawn crept over the battlefield, the valley lay strewn with the remnants of arrogance. The spoils, untouched by Zareon's hand, lay abandoned. *No riches born of war's sorrow shall taint our victory,* he vowed.

Under the early light, as Lothar's wounds were tended, silence stretched between the kindred. At last, Lothar spoke. "I chose comfort... and found chains." His voice was heavy with guilt. Zareon placed a hand on his shoulder. "Paths diverge, but grace finds those willing to return."

With captives freed and honor restored, Zareon led his men and Lothar back to Velithar. The rescue was complete—but Lothar's journey, both of soul and destiny, was far from over.

The Destruction of Ardeneth's Pride – Veyloris and Gor'maleth's Fall.

Though rescued, Lothar's return to the plains of Ardeneth was short-lived. The land, once vibrant, pulsed with a corruption deeper than greed. Cities like **Veyloris** and **Gor'maleth**—though rebuilt after war's scars—plunged into depravity worse than before. Streets that once echoed with trade now pulsed with indulgence; temples erected not to the Eternal, but to idols demanding sacrifices unthinkable. The air grew thick with the stench of sin that reached beyond mortal realms—ascending as a stench to the heavens themselves.

It was then that the Eternal's justice stirred.

One evening, beneath a sky woven with dusk and foreboding, three figures appeared before Zareon's tent. Radiance cloaked them, voices like wind through ancient trees. One spoke, "We journey to witness the cries of the plains' wickedness. The time of patience wanes. Judgment approaches."

Zareon's heart clenched. *Lothar... still among them?* He stepped forward, daring to plead. "Will You destroy the righteous with the wicked? Should there be fifty righteous... would You spare them?"

"For fifty, I shall spare the land," the voice answered.

Zareon pressed further—forty-five... forty... thirty... twenty... ten. Each plea met mercy's promise. Yet sorrow tinged the air—the darkness in those cities ran deeper than hope.

That night, as Zareon stood upon a ridge overlooking Ardeneth's distant lights, flames unseen yet kindled began to burn in the realms beyond. Messengers entered the city; warnings fell upon deaf ears. Lothar, pulled by urgency and unseen hands, fled with what remained of his household. Behind him, the city's laughter roared louder, blind to doom's breath upon their necks.

Then the heavens split open.

Fire—white-hot and merciless—rained upon Veyloris and Gor'maleth. Walls melted like wax under divine heat; stone turned to ash, bodies to shadows burned into the earth. Rivers boiled; air became flame. Screams—brief, swallowed by the inferno—echoed for but a moment before silence claimed all. The land convulsed, swallowing what once stood proud.

From Velithar's heights, Zareon beheld the pillar of smoke rising—dark, vast, stretching to the skies. His heart wept, yet his spirit stood resolute. The Eternal's justice had spoken—unyielding, pure. Beneath that smoldering ruin lay a lesson carved not in stone, but in ash: *Mercy calls, but pride silences ears.*

Lothar, breath ragged, eyes hollow, stood far beyond the destruction—alive, yet haunted. His fortune lost; his soul seared by what his choices wrought. And as dawn broke, the Sacred Realms bore witness to both wrath and grace intertwined.

For even amid ruin... the covenant endured.

Chapter 2

Eryon, the Son of the Covenant

The winds of time shift, and the chronicles of the Sacred Realms turn to a new chapter—one quieter, yet no less significant. Where Zareon's journey blazed with trials, wars, and divine encounters, the tale that follows is woven with threads of gentleness and endurance, like a steady river flowing beneath turbulent skies.

This is the saga of **Eryon**, the Son of Promise—a man whose life, though less tempestuous than his father's, carried the weight of destiny upon his shoulders. Born of a miraculous covenant and named under the canopy of starlit oaths, Eryon embodied patience, steadfastness, and quiet strength. Unlike the warriors and kings whose deeds echoed with clashing blades, Eryon's legacy was forged in the fields, in wells dug under hostile gazes, and in prayers whispered beneath ancient trees.

His was a story not of conquest, but of perseverance. Not of grand battles, but of enduring trials through unwavering faith. In the Sacred Realms, where pride often roared louder than humility, Eryon's disposition stood in stark contrast—gentle, yielding when others would fight, yet never compromising the path set before him by the Eternal.

Yet, serenity did not shield him from hardship. Famine, envy, and treacherous alliances tested him, and beneath his calm exterior burned the same divine fire that had guided Zareon. The blessings promised to his father did not end with him—they flowed through Eryon's journey, watering the roots of a lineage that would one day shake kingdoms and fulfill prophecies whispered since the dawn of creation.

As the sun sets upon Zareon's saga, it rises upon Eryon's—a tale where patience becomes might, humility becomes strength, and the covenant's promise unfolds amidst quiet fields and starlit nights. For in the Sacred Realms, not all heroes wield swords—some wield unwavering faith, and through them, the Eternal's purposes march ever forward.

Thus begins the journey of **Eryon, the Son of the Covenant**—a beacon of steadfastness in a world ever-shifting, ever-shadowed, yet ever guided by the unseen hand of the Eternal.

The Son of Promise and the Trial of Faith.

The skies of **Velithar** stretched vast and endless, the stars above shimmering like ancient sentinels bearing witness to promises spoken in the breath of the Eternal. In the tented encampment of **Zareon,** laughter—true and bright—broke through the cool night air. Sareah, long beyond the age of childbearing, cradled in her arms a miracle: a son born not of human possibility but of divine covenant. His name, **Eryon**, meaning *joyful breath*—or *laughter reborn*—reflected both the incredulity and the wonder of his arrival.

Zareon, weathered by years of wandering and trials, gazed upon his child with a tenderness that melted the weight of decades past. His hands, once calloused from battle and journey, now gently traced the infant's soft brow. *This is the promised one...* The very heir through whom the Eternal's word would flourish like the stars overhead.

Around the campfires, songs were sung of the Eternal's faithfulness, and even the herds seemed to graze more peacefully under that night's glow.

Eryon grew in strength and wisdom, his laughter a melody that lifted hearts and eased burdens. Under his father's watchful eye, he learned to tend flocks, speak with honor, and gaze at the heavens with reverence for the One who breathed worlds into being. His bond with Zareon was deep—father and son walking side by side through sun-drenched fields and along starlit ridges. Yet, beneath the serenity, a test loomed—one that would shake the foundations of faith, trust, and covenant.

One twilight, as the wind whispered through the olive trees, the Eternal's voice pierced Zareon's heart. It did not come with thunder or flame, but with a stillness so profound that it weighed heavier than any storm. *"Zareon."* His soul stirred. *"Take Eryon, your beloved son—the son of promise—and ascend to the heights of **Mount Veyloren**. There, offer him as a sacrifice."*

The world seemed to tilt, breath caught between heaven and earth. *My son... the promised one?* Conflict raged within Zareon's heart—a tempest of anguish and obedience. Yet, as he had done through countless trials, he bowed his head. *Not my will... but Yours.*

At dawn, the camp stirred as preparations unfolded. Zareon saddled his steed, gathered wood bound with leather straps, and took firestones. Eryon, ever dutiful, noticed the solemnity clouding his father's gaze but asked nothing. Two servants joined them, and together they journeyed into the wilderness.

Three days stretched long and grueling. Rocky paths tested their feet, and biting winds clawed at cloaks. Nights were spent beneath a tapestry of stars, Zareon staring upward, whispering prayers carried away by the breeze. Eryon, ever perceptive, sensed the weight in his father's silence yet chose to trust.

At last, the towering peak of **Veyloren** pierced the horizon, its summit crowned by winds that howled with ancient voices. Zareon turned to his servants. "Remain here," he said, voice steady though his soul quaked. "The boy and I shall ascend to worship... and we shall return."

Wood laden upon his back, Eryon glanced at the firestones and blade strapped to his father's belt. His curiosity broke through the stillness. "Father... we carry wood and fire, but where is the lamb for the offering?"

Zareon's steps slowed. Pain lanced through his chest, yet his answer emerged like a breath exhaled through centuries of faith. "The Eternal will provide, my son."

Their ascent was slow, each step heavy with the gravity of obedience. At the summit, winds screamed past jagged stones. Zareon, hands trembling, erected an altar of rough-hewn rocks. Each stone laid was a heartbeat of anguish, each breath a prayer. Eryon, silent now, watched with growing unease. Yet he did not resist when his father turned to him, tears glistening in his eyes.

Gently, Zareon explained—words thick with sorrow. "My son... you are the offering."

And in that moment, the world seemed to hold its breath. Yet Eryon, born of promise and raised in trust, did not flee. He lay upon the altar, gaze fixed upon the sky. *If this is the Eternal's will... then so be it.*

Zareon lifted the blade, his hand shaking with the weight of choice and destiny. His heart cried out in silent agony: *Eternal One, must this be so?* The blade poised, breath held—time itself stretched into eternity.

Then—like a torrent breaking through dammed rivers—the voice of the Eternal roared: *"Zareon! Stay your hand! Do not harm the boy. Now I know you fear Me, for you have not withheld even your beloved son."*

Relief crashed through Zareon as he dropped the blade, collapsing beside Eryon. Tears—of gratitude, of release—poured forth. Then, caught in a nearby thicket, a **ram with horns entwined in branches** appeared—a providence none could deny. Together, father and son offered the ram, smoke curling upward in worship and thanksgiving.

As the embers glowed and the skies seemed to shimmer brighter, the Eternal's voice spoke once more: *"Because you have obeyed without reservation, I shall bless you beyond measure. Your descendants will be as countless as the stars you gaze upon and the grains beneath your feet. Through your lineage, all realms shall be blessed."*

Descending from **Mount Veyloren**, Zareon's steps felt lighter, Eryon walking beside him—silent, contemplative, yet alive with renewed understanding. The stars above, ancient and ever-watching, gleamed like a thousand affirmations.

The test had been given. Faith had been proven. And the covenant, etched now not just in promise but in the marrow of their souls, burned brighter than ever.

In the Sacred Realms, obedience to the Eternal was not without cost—but its reward echoed beyond the span of lifetimes, into eternities yet unseen.

The Binding of Destinies – Eryon and Serenya.

The Sacred Realms, with their sprawling mountains and windswept plains, stood at a crossroads of destiny. **Eryon**, now a man of forty winters, walked the lands of **Velithar** with steadfastness, his every step guided by the covenant forged through his father, **Zareon**. His life, though marked with peace, bore a quiet longing—he was the son of promise, yet his lineage stood at the brink of continuation. Without an heir, the covenant's future hung suspended like stars waiting to fall.

Zareon, aged yet unwavering in spirit, summoned his most trusted servant, **Elam**, a man seasoned by years and faithful beyond question. His beard, silvered with time, bore witness to journeys across deserts, mountains, and courts of kings. "Elam," Zareon spoke under the shadow of an ancient oak, "swear by the Eternal, the Maker of skies and seas, that you will not take a wife for my son from the peoples of these lands whose ways wander from truth. Go instead to my kin in **Arvandor**, the highlands of my forefathers, and seek from them a bride for Eryon."

Elam placed a weathered hand upon Zareon's sword-hilt—a solemn oath—and nodded. "By the breath of the Eternal, I shall do as you command."

Preparations unfolded swiftly. Ten camels, adorned with embroidered saddlebags heavy with precious gifts—silver chalices, golden armlets, and fine fabrics shimmering like rivers beneath moonlight—were readied. Elam mounted, flanked by servants, and they departed at dawn. The journey stretched across unforgiving sands of the **Vastmere Expanse**, where scorching winds howled like spirits in anguish, and nights were cloaked in chilling silence beneath constellations that whispered of old promises.

Days bled into weeks until the distant hills of **Arvandor** pierced the horizon. Lush valleys stretched beyond, and the city of **Myrren's Port** gleamed with towering spires and bustling markets scented with spice and cedar. Elam's heart, though resolute, carried the weight of uncertainty. *How shall I know whom the Eternal has chosen?* he pondered. Dismounting near a well that glistened like liquid crystal beneath the setting sun, he knelt, pressing his palm into the earth.

With eyes lifted to the heavens, he prayed: "O Eternal, God of my master Zareon, guide my steps. Let it be that the maiden who offers me water and tends to my camels without request—let her be the one You have appointed for Eryon."

Even as his words faded into the cooling breeze, footsteps approached—light, yet assured. Turning, Elam beheld her: a maiden whose presence seemed to still the world around her. Her hair cascaded like midnight waves, eyes reflecting the deep azure of distant lakes. Draped in robes embroidered with symbols of her clan, she carried an earthen jar balanced upon a slender shoulder.

"Drink, my lord," she offered, voice like a gentle stream. Elam, heart quickening, sipped gratefully. Without pause, she lowered her jar and drew water for his camels, working with swift grace as the beasts drank their fill. *Surely this is no mere chance,* he thought, wonder blooming within.

When the camels' thirst was quenched, Elam spoke: "Pray, tell me, whose daughter are you?"

"I am **Serenya**, daughter of **Bethaniel**, son of Naharon," she replied. Her words struck like a chord of destiny—kin of Zareon's house. Overcome, Elam produced a golden bracelet, sliding it upon her wrist, and adorned her with earrings crafted like woven stars. "Blessed be the Eternal, who has not withheld His steadfast love."

Serenya, cheeks flushed with surprise and wonder, hastened back to her family's dwelling. Bethaniel, hearing her tale and seeing the adornments, welcomed Elam and his company into his halls where torches cast warm light upon stone walls etched with ancestral stories. Feasts were prepared—lamb roasted with herbs, bread steaming from stone ovens—and wine flowed as tales were exchanged. Yet Elam, ever mindful of his mission, spoke plainly after the meal: "I am a servant of Zareon. My master sent me to seek a bride for his son. Upon praying at the well, the Eternal answered swiftly through Serenya's kindness. If you grant her hand, we shall depart at dawn."

Bethaniel and his kin exchanged glances, the weight of the moment settling over them like a soft fog. Yet Serenya, eyes alight with both trepidation and an undeniable pull toward destiny, spoke first: "I will go." Her voice, though gentle, bore unwavering resolve—a willingness to step beyond the familiar into the unknown, carried by faith in the Eternal's weaving hand.

The next morning, with farewells kissed upon cheeks and prayers whispered like wind-borne blessings, the caravan set forth. Serenya rode beneath a canopy of silks, heart pounding with every hoofbeat. Miles stretched behind; destiny beckoned ahead.

As the sun dipped toward the horizon of **Velithar**, casting the landscape in amber hues, Eryon walked alone through the fields—lost in thought, prayers murmured to the wind. Looking up, he saw the procession crest a distant hill. His heart stilled, breath catching as golden light framed the figures like a painting come to life.

Serenya, veiled yet radiant, dismounted. Eryon approached, their eyes meeting across a breathless span of space and time. Questions unspoken. Answers unnecessary. In that gaze, trust blossomed, and destiny solidified.

Beneath the ancient skies, with the wind singing through cypress groves and the stars beginning their silent vigil, Eryon took

Serenya's hand. A tent was prepared, lanterns casting soft glow, as vows were exchanged—not in grand halls, but under the watchful gaze of the Eternal and the infinite tapestry above.

Their union was not merely a binding of hearts but of purpose. Through laughter, tears, and countless dawns, their love would kindle hope across generations. And as they stood together that night, arms entwined, the Sacred Realms seemed to exhale—a promise carried forward through them, shining brighter than any star overhead.

The Rival Sons – Kaelen and Darion.

The lands of **Velithar**, with their sprawling meadows and jagged cliffs, echoed with the cries of new life. In the tent of **Eryon** and **Serenya**, under the canopy of a starlit sky, two sons were born—twins whose destinies would intertwine with tension, ambition, and prophecy. Yet from the very beginning, the air between them seemed charged with unseen conflict, as if the Eternal had woven into their beings the threads of a rivalry that would shape generations.

The first to emerge was **Kaelen**, his skin ruddy, his hair a wild cascade the color of embers. His tiny fists clenched as if already grappling with the world, and his cries were fierce, reverberating through the camp like a war horn. No sooner had he been lifted to the sky in blessing than his brother followed—**Darion**, grasping Kaelen's heel, his touch firm, as if refusing to let his elder brother claim precedence unchallenged. Darion's gaze, even as an infant, carried an unsettling calm—dark eyes reflecting depths far beyond his years.

Eryon held both sons in his arms, pride swelling like the rivers of **Elyndor** after spring rains. Yet even then, **Serenya** sensed the brewing storm beneath their shared blood. "Two nations war within them," she whispered to her husband one moonlit night, recalling the words spoken to her in prayerful visions. "One shall rise over the other... but not without cost."

Years unfurled like rolling waves, and the boys grew beneath the watchful gaze of the Sacred Realms. Kaelen became a force of nature—broad-shouldered, quick to laughter yet quicker to anger. He roamed the wilds, bow slung across his back, his footsteps light despite his imposing frame. The forests became his sanctuary, the hunt his domain. His arms bore scars from beasts slain and cliffs scaled. Around campfires, stories of his exploits spread: how he felled a mountain lion with a single arrow, how he waded into rivers to wrestle stags. He thrived on adrenaline, his spirit a blaze uncontainable.

Darion, in contrast, favored the quiet places—those where the wind whispered through tents and ancient texts lay unrolled upon woven mats. Where Kaelen's world was the thrill of pursuit, Darion's was the art of patience. His hands, though slender, were deft; he bartered shrewdly in markets, his words weaving circles around merchants. He studied the stars, learned the secrets of herbs, and knew how to speak so that hearts softened—or hardened at his will. In his presence, people found themselves revealing truths they hadn't meant to share.

Eryon's affection gravitated toward Kaelen—admiring his strength, his bravery, his reflection of the raw world beyond the tents. To Eryon, Kaelen embodied the vigor of the Sacred Realms, the defender of lineage and land. He would often clasp his eldest son on the shoulder, pride radiating like the morning sun.

Serenya, however, saw in Darion a different kind of strength—a quiet fire that burned no less fiercely. She marveled at his intuition, his ability to read not just words but souls. "Kaelen may conquer fields," she would muse, "but Darion... Darion conquers hearts." Her favor was no secret; she defended him when camp disputes arose, praised his counsel during decisions. Their bond was woven through shared conversations beneath starlit skies and mornings spent gathering herbs in the glades.

The brothers' contrasting natures bred friction like flint striking steel. Kaelen mocked Darion's penchant for caution. "You spend your days among pots and scrolls while the world roars beyond the tents! Life isn't meant to be measured in words, brother, but in scars!" Darion, unfazed, would reply, "And yet, brother, scars can blind a man just as easily as pride. The world isn't conquered by brawn alone."

Their quarrels grew sharper as their strengths did. Kaelen's hunts returned with greater spoils, earning him the admiration of their clan. Darion's shrewd dealings filled their stores with riches that Kaelen's hunts could not match. At feasts, Kaelen's voice boomed with tales of beasts slain; Darion's wit drew laughter from the elders.

But beneath the surface, jealousy simmered. Kaelen resented how Darion's words could sway even their father's decisions. Darion, for his part, envied Kaelen's easy acceptance into Eryon's proud gaze. Their rivalry, once playful, deepened into something darker—each footstep taken shadowed by competition.

The camp of Eryon became a household divided. Kaelen sat beside his father, sharpening blades beneath the open sky, stories of conquest binding them in shared glory. Darion, seated beside Serenya within the tent, poured over maps and scrolls, his mother's fingers absently tracing his hair as they discussed future lands and promised blessings.

The Sacred Realms watched in silence as destiny's tapestry stretched taut between the two brothers. Bonds of blood pulled against the weight of favor, ambition gnawed at love's foundation, and the

Eternal's unseen hand guided events toward a reckoning neither Kaelen nor Darion could foresee.

For in the shadow of rivalry... choices awaited. Choices that would shape kingdoms, divide legacies, and echo beyond the lifespans of both hunter and schemer.

Shadows Over Gerathen – The Trial of Fear and Favor.

The lands of **Velithar** grew parched beneath a sky that withheld its rain. Fields, once lush with golden grain and emerald pastures, shriveled under the relentless gaze of the sun. Rivers thinned to mere trickles; wells turned to dust. Hunger crept across the land, clawing at every village and encampment. In the face of this desolation, **Eryon**— charged with shepherding not only flocks but the covenant bestowed upon him—made a choice that would lead him into lands shadowed by both peril and promise.

Gathering his household, herds, and servants, Eryon journeyed westward, toward the kingdom of **Gerathen**—a realm known for its fertile valleys and fortified cities. Whispers among travelers spoke of King **Abimareth**, a ruler whose justice was as swift as his temper was unpredictable. Yet desperation drove Eryon onward. *If famine claims us, the covenant's lineage falters,* he reasoned.

Upon approaching the stone walls of **Veylor Keep**, the heart of Gerathen, Eryon's gaze shifted to **Serenya**. Even beneath the travel-worn cloak draped over her shoulders, her beauty shone—a radiance untouched by the journey's hardships. Concern shadowed his features. *The eyes of this court... they will notice her.* Fear, an unwelcome visitor, gripped his heart. Would foreign desires and ambitions threaten what he cherished most?

Turning to Serenya, his voice dropped to a whisper. "Say that you are my sister," he urged. "If they covet you as my wife, envy may breed murder. This deception... it is but a shield against their malice."

Serenya's eyes searched his—hesitation flickering—but trust prevailed. *Better to live under the weight of hidden truth than to fall to the sword of ambition.* She nodded.

Their arrival in Gerathen's court did not go unnoticed. Richly adorned courtiers and iron-clad guards observed them with a mix of curiosity and veiled greed. Eryon's caravan, laden with herds and servants, was unlike any the city had recently seen—a traveling prince cloaked in foreign dust.

Among the crowd, the gazes most intense were directed at Serenya. Whispers rippled through the air: *Who is this woman whose grace rivals the morning sun?* Offers and glances laced with hidden motives circulated like smoke curling through a banquet hall.

Eryon's deception worked—at first. His "sister" was treated with a respect tinged with desire, and no immediate threat arose. Yet truth has a way of seeping through even the strongest of walls. Days turned to weeks, and sharp-eyed servants noticed the subtle touches, the glances exchanged between husband and wife when they thought no eyes watched. Questions grew like storm clouds gathering on the horizon.

It was King Abimareth himself, a man draped in crimson robes and crowned with onyx and silver, who unveiled the truth. One morning, from his palace balcony overlooking the city square, he glimpsed Eryon and Serenya—laughter shared between them, a fleeting gesture of intimacy undeniable to any who saw. The king's eyes narrowed. *Lies dressed in silk are still lies.*

Summoning Eryon to his court, Abimareth's voice thundered through the gilded hall. "What is this treachery? You spoke of a sister, yet your hands tell another tale. Did you think Gerathen's halls blind? Speak!"

Eryon's heart pounded, yet he stood tall. "I feared for my life," he admitted. "Her beauty is such that I thought deceit safer than truth."

A tense silence hung like a blade suspended over them all. Then Abimareth, gaze stern but tempered with reason, addressed the assembly: "Who among you dares harm this man or his wife shall answer with blood—yours forfeit upon Gerathen's stones! Let no hand nor whisper seek to claim what is not theirs." His decree rang out, echoing through every corridor and market stall. The people, wary of their king's wrath, backed away—grudgingly respectful.

Yet peace birthed another form of conflict. As Eryon sowed crops and tended herds, the Eternal's blessing poured forth like rain on parched ground. His fields flourished beyond reason; his flocks multiplied beyond measure. Wealth flowed into his hands as rivers flood their banks after a storm. His tents stretched across the plains, a veritable kingdom in motion.

But prosperity stirs envy like carrion draws vultures. The people of Gerathen, once hospitable, began to mutter darkly. *Why should a foreigner reap where we toil?* Wells that Eryon's servants dug were seized. Fields were sabotaged under moonlight. Stones shattered clay jars, and curses hissed through clenched teeth as neighbors turned to adversaries.

Abimareth, torn between respecting the covenant-bearer and quelling unrest among his people, called Eryon once more. His expression was weighed with reluctant authority. "Your presence breeds discord, not by your fault, but by hearts poisoned with jealousy. Depart, lest peace unravel entirely."

Though stung by rejection, Eryon bowed. "I hold no quarrel with Gerathen nor with you, my lord. I shall go."

Gathering his household, he journeyed southward toward the borderlands of **Bevrath**. Beneath the vast expanse of starlit heavens, he pitched his tents upon an open plain near ancient wells whose waters ran deep. There, beneath gnarled oaks and silver-clouded skies, Eryon knelt. An altar of stones was raised, flames licking upward as a symbol of thanksgiving.

And it was there that the Eternal appeared to him once more— voice a balm to the wounds of exile: *"Fear not, Eryon. I am with you. My covenant endures. In you and your seed, My promise shall flourish."*

Comfort washed over him like morning light breaking through lingering night clouds. His heart, bruised by persecution and deception's weight, steadied. Despite man's envy and the shifting tides of fortune, the Eternal's favor remained steadfast—an anchor against the storms.

Thus, under a sky ablaze with stars countless as the promises spoken over him, Eryon stood tall. *Man's rejection is fleeting,* he thought, *but the Eternal's word is eternal.*

And so, the chapter of Gerathen closed not in defeat, but with a blessing carried onward by footsteps guided by divine hand—toward horizons yet to be claimed, toward destinies yet to unfold.

Chapter 3

Darion and the Twelve Scions

The Sacred Realms, ever shifting beneath the gaze of the Eternal, stood at the threshold of a new era. With the passing of generations, the covenant first whispered beneath star-laden skies to Zareon and carried through Eryon now flowed through **Darion**, a man whose life would be marked by ambition, struggle, and the forging of legacies destined to shape the fate of realms.

But destiny rarely unfolds without the weaving of hardship and shadow. Darion's journey would be a tapestry stretched between deceit and redemption, exile and restoration. He was a man of wit and cunning, whose choices—born of both desperation and determination—would ripple across lands and lifetimes. In the crucible of his trials, twelve sons would be born, each bearing the seed of a future tribe. These scions, bound by blood yet divided by rivalry, would lay the foundation of nations, their names etched into history through valor, betrayal, and the hand of providence.

This is a tale of shifting allegiances and tumultuous hearts—of journeys into foreign lands where deception thrives, and alliances are forged upon uncertain ground. It is the story of love found and lost, of labor under oppressive hands, of dreams that span from the dust of the earth to the highest heavens. Amid the discord of brothers and the weight of choices, the Eternal's plan moved like a hidden river, carving paths unseen yet unstoppable.

Darion's saga is not one of ease. His road is marked by longing—for blessing, for belonging, for peace within a heart torn by ambition and destiny's call. And through his life, the Sacred Realms would witness the birth of twelve legacies, twelve banners that would one day march upon the pages of prophecy and the fields of fate.

Thus begins the chronicle of **Darion and the Twelve Scions**—a story where the bonds of family are both shield and blade, and where the Eternal's hand, though sometimes hidden in shadow, guides all toward a destiny none could foresee.

The Veiled Deception and the Stolen Blessing.

The passage of time weighs heavily upon all mortals, and none were exempt—not even **Eryon**, the bearer of the covenant. His once-keen eyes, which had gazed upon horizons ablaze with promise, now clouded like mist over distant mountains. His strength waned; his breath, once firm, grew shallow. The sands of his life slipped through unseen fingers, and with them came the urgency to pass on the mantle of blessing—a legacy birthed in divine promise and destined to shape the Sacred Realms.

In the vast encampment nestled between the rolling hills of **Bevrath**, Eryon summoned his eldest son, **Kaelen**—hunter of the wilds, his beard thick and hands scarred from years of wrestling beasts and weather. His father's voice, though frail, carried the weight of authority. "My son," Eryon rasped, "the time draws near for me to depart this realm. Fetch your bow, your quiver—go to the fields and hunt. Prepare for me the savory meal I so cherish, that my soul may bless you before I pass beyond the veil."

Kaelen's chest swelled with pride. This was the moment—the culmination of birthright, of years spent earning his father's favor.

Without hesitation, he slung his weathered bow across his back and strode into the wilderness, the promise of inheritance burning in his heart like a torch against the dark.

But shadows stirred beyond Kaelen's steps. Behind the canvas walls of their tent, **Serenya**—mother, matriarch, and silent strategist—had listened. Her heart, divided between love for both sons, leaned toward **Darion**: the son of contemplation, the son whose dreams reached beyond fields and prey into realms of promise. Had not the Eternal whispered to her in earlier days, *"The elder shall serve the younger"*? Was destiny to be left to mere chance... or claimed through decisive action?

Pulling Darion aside, Serenya's gaze—sharp as a blade's edge—locked with his. "Your father sends Kaelen to the wilds to prepare for the blessing. We cannot let this pass. Remember the agreement between you and your brother—he sold you the birthright for fleeting hunger. That exchange, though dismissed by him, carries weight. Yet words spoken over bread and stew will not suffice; the blessing must be claimed."

Darion's brow furrowed. His nature leaned toward patience, not deceit, yet ambition flickered beneath the surface—a hunger not easily ignored. *To be the heir... to be the vessel through which the Eternal's promise flows...* The stakes towered like the peaks of **Mount Veyloren**.

Serenya's plan unfurled like a tapestry woven with both wisdom and danger. "Go quickly," she urged, "select two young goats from the herd. I shall prepare them as your father desires. Wear Kaelen's garments—the ones scented with the forests and fields he roams. His musk clings to them. I will drape your arms with the skins of the goats; your father's touch will find the roughness it expects. Speak carefully, for his hearing sharpens where his sight fails."

Darion's heartbeat quickened as he slipped into his brother's weathered tunic, the fabric smelling of pine, sweat, and the open wilds. The goat hides, coarse against his skin, wrapped around his arms. Serenya's hands—steady and sure—adjusted his disguise, her eyes dark pools of determination. "Go now," she whispered. "Delay, and all is lost."

Within the inner tent, the air hung heavy with the scent of roasted meat and smoldering incense. Eryon reclined upon woven mats, his face a map of lines carved by years of journey and promise. His blind eyes gazed into a realm beyond sight as Darion entered, carrying the platter.

"My father," Darion spoke, voice lowered to mimic Kaelen's gruff timbre, "I am here. I have hunted as you asked. Eat, that your soul may bless me."

Eryon's milky gaze turned toward the sound. Doubt flickered like a brief shadow across his face. "How... how did you find game so swiftly, my son?"

Darion's pulse thudded, yet he pressed on. "The Eternal—your God—granted me success," he answered, the words tasting like ash upon his tongue.

Still, uncertainty gnawed at Eryon. His hand reached out, calloused fingers seeking truth through touch. He grasped Darion's arm—the goat hides rough beneath his palm—confirming what his ears strained to believe. "The voice is Darion's," he muttered, "yet the hands... the hands are Kaelen's."

Lifting a portion of the prepared meal, Eryon ate. The familiar flavors—rich, seasoned perfectly—lulled his suspicions. He leaned closer, inhaling. *Yes... the scent of the fields... my son, the hunter...*

"Come near," Eryon commanded, and Darion obeyed. Hands trembling, Eryon laid his fingers upon his son's head. His voice, frail yet laced with ancient authority, rose into the tent's dim air:

"May the Eternal grant you the dew of the heavens and the richness of the earth, abundance of grain and new wine. Nations shall serve you, and peoples bow before you. Be lord over your kin, and may those who curse you be cursed, and those who bless you be blessed."

The words poured forth like a river breaking free of stone confines—once spoken, irrevocable. A blessing sealed by heaven itself.

Darion stepped back, heart pounding with a maelstrom of guilt and triumph. *It is done.*

Moments later, footsteps thudded outside. The flap tore open—**Kaelen** entered, garments dusted with the wilderness, quiver empty yet face alight with expectation. "Father," he called, "rise and eat of my catch, that your soul may bless me!"

Silence—thick and oppressive—coiled through the tent. Eryon's face drained of color. "Who...?" His voice broke, realization dawning like a thunderstorm cresting the mountains. "Who... was it that came before you? I ate... and blessed him... and indeed, he is blessed."

Kaelen's joy crumbled into fury. Rage twisted his features as his roar shook the tent walls. "Darion!" he bellowed, fists clenching like coiled vipers. "He has deceived me! He has stolen what was mine!"

Desperation clawed at Kaelen's throat. "Father, have you but one blessing? Bless me, too!"

But Eryon's head bowed under the weight of words already spoken. "Your brother came deceitfully," he murmured. "And he has taken the blessing."

Kaelen's eyes burned with wrath and bitterness. His voice, dark with promise, spat forth, "The days of mourning for my father draw near... and then... then I shall kill my brother."

Outside, winds howled over the plains, carrying with them the seeds of what had been sown—deception, ambition, and a destiny now set into motion. Bloodlines would be strained. Paths would diverge. Yet the tapestry woven by the Eternal would endure, threads of shadow and light interlaced by hands beyond mortal grasp.

And so, Darion, the younger, now bore the weight of blessing— and the burden of enmity that would chase him across realms. Choices made in a moment would echo across generations. Destiny was claimed... but not without cost.

The Twilight of Eryon – Brothers Reunited in Mourning.

Time, like an ever-flowing river, carries even the greatest of men toward the shores of their final breath. **Eryon**, the son of promise and bearer of the covenant's weight, lived long beyond the span of most mortal men. Seasons ebbed and flowed; kingdoms rose and crumbled, yet his life endured—a living testament to the Eternal's favor. His hair, once the hue of darkened wheat, turned to silver streams; his gaze, though clouded with age, still held the remnants of the steadfastness that had defined him.

As his final days approached, Eryon's tent stood still upon the plains of **Bevrath**, the winds soft and reverent as if the very land paid homage. Within its folds, the aged patriarch reclined upon woven silks, his breaths slow but resolute. By his side stood **Serenya**, her hands worn from the years but ever gentle as she offered water to parched lips. Eryon's eyes, dulled by time, turned skyward. *The stars... the same canopy beneath which the Eternal spoke to me. How many promises sealed in their light? How many yet to unfold?*

Word of Eryon's waning strength spread like mist across the Sacred Realms, reaching the ears of his sons—**Kaelen**, the hunter whose footsteps echoed through forests and battlefields, and **Darion**, the wanderer and schemer, weathered by journeys and wrestling's of both body and spirit. The gulf between them, forged by years of rivalry and betrayal, weighed heavily upon them. Yet, as the shadow of death stretched over their father's tent, pride gave way to the unyielding pull of blood and memory.

Kaelen arrived first—his cloak heavy with dust, his face carved with lines of hardship and hard-won battles. He stood at the entrance, hesitation flickering across his fierce gaze. Not long after, Darion approached, his steps measured, robes trailing behind him like whispers of the past. Their eyes met—tension sparking like flint against steel— but neither spoke of old wounds. There, beneath the looming weight of impending loss, rivalry was eclipsed by the simple truth: they were sons. And their father was dying.

Within the dim tent, Eryon's voice—a mere shadow of its former timbre—broke the silence. "My sons... you have come." His hand, trembling, reached for them. Kaelen knelt first, his rugged hand engulfing his fathers in a grip both strong and tender. Darion followed, his touch lighter, eyes misted with emotions he dared not voice. "Remember... the covenant," Eryon whispered, gaze shifting between them. "Not by strength alone... nor by cunning... but by the Eternal's hand shall you endure."

The final breath came with the fading light of dusk—a sigh that seemed to echo beyond the confines of flesh, releasing a soul into realms unseen. Outside, the winds rose, swirling dust and petals alike— a tribute offered by the very world he had walked.

According to the customs of their lineage, Kaelen and Darion set aside their past enmity, their movements in somber harmony as they prepared Eryon's body. Fine linens, perfumed with myrrh and althaea petals, wrapped his form. His staff—marked with carvings of journeys past—was placed beside him, a symbol of both his leadership and unwavering faith. Word spread across Velithar and beyond; chieftains, elders, and distant kin gathered, their faces reflecting the solemnity of the moment.

Together, the brothers bore the bier upon which their father rested. The journey to the **Vale of Makhareth**, where the tomb of their grandfather **Zareon** lay carved into the heart of a limestone hill, was marked by silence—broken only by the mournful notes of reed flutes and the steady beat of drums echoing through the valleys. Along the path, villagers and travelers paused, bowing their heads in respect. Children gazed in wonder, elders in reverent memory.

Upon reaching the mouth of the tomb, torches flickered, casting warm light upon the ancient stone, its arch etched with runes proclaiming the legacy of those buried within. Kaelen, eyes fierce yet glistening with unshed tears, and Darion, face shadowed with contemplation, carried their father into the depths of the chamber. Beside the resting place of Zareon and **Sareah**, Eryon was laid to rest—his journey complete, his soul commended to the Eternal.

Kaelen turned away; shoulders tense. "He was... a better man than I understood," he muttered. Darion glanced at his brother, the edges of old wounds softening. "He bore the weight of us both," he replied quietly. "And still stood steadfast."

As they emerged from the tomb into the open air, night stretched above, the stars burning bright—points of light unchanged by the passage of men. Under that celestial tapestry, Kaelen and Darion stood side by side. No words of reconciliation were spoken, none needed. Their shared loss forged a fleeting bridge across years of discord—a reminder that blood, despite strife, binds in ways time cannot sever.

The Sacred Realms, ever watching, bore witness to the end of an era and the beginning of another. With Eryon's passing, the covenant's torch passed fully to the next generation. Choices awaited, destinies unfurled, and the Eternal's hand continued to guide unseen.

Yet, for that night, beneath the ancient sky, there was only silence, memory, and the quiet unity of two sons honoring a father's legacy.

The Exile of Darion – Flight, Bonds, and Fortune.

The echoes of betrayal lingered in the halls of **Bevrath**, seeping into its stone and soil. **Kaelen's** fury burned like an untamed blaze, his wrath a storm that no mortal wall could restrain. Word of his vow—*"I shall not rest until Darion's blood stains the earth!"*—spread swiftly through the lands, carried by wind and tongue alike. With death's shadow looming ever closer, **Darion**, the bearer of a stolen blessing and a heart tangled in guilt and ambition, fled into the night.

His departure was shrouded in haste and sorrow. **Serenya**, his mother, pressed into his palm a satchel filled with dried meats and herbs, her hands lingering on his face. "Go to my kin in the northern reaches of **Haranthal**," she urged, voice thick with emotion. "There, you will find sanctuary in the house of **Lethan**. And perhaps... in time, Kaelen's wrath will cool." Darion nodded, swallowing the knot of fear and regret that lodged in his throat. Behind him, the fires of his home flickered against the darkness—comfort turned memory.

The journey northward was treacherous. Vast stretches of barren plains yielded to jagged hills where howling winds clawed at his cloak. Nights offered no rest; his dreams twisted with visions of Kaelen's burning gaze, of a blade flashing beneath moonlight. Hunger gnawed, and thirst parched his throat, yet he pressed on. *To stop is to die.* But amidst the bleakness, fate—woven by the Eternal's unseen hand—laid a path.

On the seventh night, wearied beyond measure, Darion sought shelter among a cluster of ancient stones. There, beneath the vast expanse of stars, he lay upon a rock, the heavens stretched like a canvas ablaze with celestial fire. And as sleep claimed him, the Eternal whispered through dream and vision. He beheld a towering stairway—a luminous bridge—stretching from earth to the realms above. Ethereal beings ascended and descended its length, radiant figures moving with purpose. Above it all, a voice—resounding like the clash of mountains and the gentlest of rivers—spoke:

"Darion, son of Eryon... though you flee, My hand is upon you. The land upon which you rest shall be yours and your descendants'. Through you, all realms shall be blessed. I shall not forsake you until My promise is fulfilled."

Darion awoke, breath catching in his chest, the vision etched into his soul. Erecting a stone pillar, he anointed it with oil from his satchel, murmuring, "This place... this is the **Threshold of the Heavens**." Strength renewed; he pressed onward.

Weeks later, dust-laden and travel-worn, Darion crested a ridge overlooking a fertile valley, where verdant pastures unfurled beneath rolling mists. At its heart, wells dotted the landscape, shepherds tending flocks that roamed like clouds upon the earth. It was there—by a well encircled by smooth stones—that destiny's next thread wove into place.

A young woman approached, her steps light but purposeful, a jar resting upon her shoulder. Her eyes—clear as the Silver Pools of **Merith**—met his, curiosity flickering within their depths. "Who are you, traveler?" she asked, voice like wind through reeds.

"I seek the house of Lethan," Darion replied. "My mother is of his kin."

The woman's gaze softened. "I am **Rhaelen**, daughter of Lethan." A smile—warm and genuine—curved her lips. "Come. You are welcome."

Led to her father's hearth, Darion recounted his tale—of flight, of vision, of seeking sanctuary. Lethan, a man whose years had carved wisdom into his face, welcomed him with open arms. "Blood calls to blood," he said. "You shall find shelter here."

Time, like the steady flow of rivers, carried Darion deeper into Haranthal's embrace. Days were spent tending flocks under blazing suns and frigid nights, learning the rhythms of shepherding and trade. Yet amidst labor's toil, his heart gravitated toward Rhaelen—her laughter a melody that lingered, her kindness a balm to his restless soul. Love blossomed like wildflowers after rain. Approaching Lethan, Darion spoke plainly, "Let me wed your daughter. Name your price."

Lethan's gaze measured him. "Serve me seven cycles of harvest and sowing," he said. Without hesitation, Darion agreed.

Years unfurled. The days were grueling—chasing stray goats across cliffs, defending herds from prowling beasts whose eyes gleamed with hunger. His hands, once soft with cunning, grew calloused with honest work. Yet each sunset, with Rhaelen's voice greeting him at the gates, made the burden light.

At the end of seven years, a grand feast was held beneath starlit skies. Lanterns swayed on silken cords, casting amber glow upon merriment and song. Veiled and adorned, Rhaelen was led to Darion. That night, vows whispered, and hands entwined, joy seemed complete.

Yet morning revealed a cruel twist—Lethan, cunning in his own right, had veiled **Liraen**, Rhaelen's elder sister, beneath the ceremonial shroud. Darion's fury blazed. "Why deceive me?" he demanded.

"It is not our custom," Lethan replied coolly, "for the younger to wed before the elder. Serve another seven cycles, and Rhaelen shall be yours."

Anger warred with love, but Darion—driven by desire and destiny—agreed. Seven more years passed. Seasons turned fields from green to gold and back again. At last, Rhaelen became his wife truly, their union celebrated with less grandeur but deeper sincerity.

With time, Darion's flocks multiplied beyond reckoning. Goats bore twins; ewes birthed without fail. His herds spread like the Vastmere Expanse beneath moonlit skies. Wealth flowed, yet with prosperity came tension. Lethan's sons grumbled—*"He takes what should be ours!"*—envy seeping like poison through familial bonds.

Darion, though enriched, found peace elusive. Dreams haunted him—Kaelen's face, distant lands calling. *How long can a man prosper where hearts turn cold against him?*

And so, after two decades woven with love, labor, and deceit's shadow, Darion's gaze turned southward—toward Velithar, toward home... toward unfinished reckonings.

But the Sacred Realms stirred with more than just the journey of one man. Behind flocks and fortunes, the Eternal's hand moved still— guiding, shaping, preparing the next great turning of destiny's wheel.

The Road of Reckoning – Darion's Return to Velithar.

Two decades had passed since **Darion** fled the wrath of his brother **Kaelen**, seeking refuge in the distant highlands of **Haranthal**. In those years, the boy who had deceived for blessing had become a man marked by love, hardship, and the burdens of wealth amassed through toil and cunning. His herds now stretched beyond counting, his tents sprawling like a nomadic kingdom across the valley plains. Yet prosperity brought not peace. Whispers of envy curled like smoke around the campfires of his kin, and the gaze of his father-in-law, **Lethan**, once warm, had cooled with suspicion.

The tension grew thick as storm clouds. Lethan's sons muttered curses, their glances daggers. *"He has taken what should be ours,"* they hissed. *"Look how the Eternal's favor rests upon a foreigner!"* Livestock that once roamed freely now became points of contention. Accusations of theft, deceit, and betrayal laced every conversation. Lethan, caught between kinship and pride, confronted Darion beneath the shadow of the olive groves.

"You have taken my daughters, my wealth... What remains mine?" Lethan's voice, once a father's counsel, was now edged with bitterness.

Darion, heart heavy with weariness, replied, "I served you with no deceit in my hands. What I have is not stolen—it is the fruit of my labor, blessed by the Eternal." Yet his words fell upon ears hardened by resentment.

That night, as Darion pondered beneath a canopy of stars, a familiar presence stirred the stillness. In a dream, the Eternal spoke once more: *"Rise. Depart from this land. Return to the soil of your fathers, to the land of promise. I am with you."*

Morning's first light found Darion standing before his wives, **Rhaelen** and **Liraen**, his voice resolute. "We leave at dawn. The time has come." There was no protest. Both had witnessed the shifting winds. The encampment buzzed with activity—tents dismantled, livestock herded, belongings secured. Children clung to their mothers as the caravan, vast and laden with the weight of both wealth and destiny, stretched toward the horizon.

Their flight was veiled in secrecy. By moonlight, they crossed the rolling hills and winding paths of Haranthal, seeking to outrun Lethan's wrath. Yet rumors travel swifter than feet. It was not long before dust rose behind them—horsemen, fierce and relentless, bearing down upon the fleeing caravan. At their head rode Lethan, face stern, eyes ablaze with indignation.

They converged in a barren valley where the wind howled through jagged stones. Darion stood between his family and the advancing host, heart pounding but gaze unyielding. Tension crackled like dry branches ready to ignite.

But before words could become swords, Lethan spoke—his voice, though sharp, carried something deeper beneath the anger. "Why did you flee in secret, like a thief in the night? Did you think I would harm my daughters... my grandchildren? You denied me the chance to bid farewell."

Darion's shoulders eased. "I feared your anger. And the gods of your land—idols not mine—compelled me to seek the path the Eternal has laid before me."

The exchange could have fractured further, but the Eternal's hand guided hearts. Cooler words followed heated ones. Pride gave way to understanding. There, amidst the wind and rock, they erected a stone pillar—**Gal'eneth**, the Witness Stone—a boundary and a covenant. "May the Eternal watch between us," Lethan declared, "that neither I cross to harm you, nor you to harm me."

Darion nodded. "We part not as enemies but as men who have shared burdens and blessings alike."

Parting was bittersweet. As Lethan and his sons rode away, Rhaelen cast a lingering glance toward her homeland. *Farewell to what was... and to what must now be left behind.*

The road south was long and fraught with the weight of anticipation. Darion's heart was torn between relief and dread. *Kaelen... will he still seek my life?* Memories of betrayal, of anger that burned hotter than a forge's fire, haunted every mile.

Then, one dusk as copper hues bled across the sky, scouts returned with grim news: Kaelen approached—with four hundred men. Not travelers. Not merchants. An army. Fear clawed at Darion's chest. *This is no welcome... it is reckoning.*

That night, campfires flickered like scattered stars. Darion withdrew alone into the wilderness, his thoughts a tempest. *Has everything led to ruin? Must I lose all to the blade of vengeance?* Dropping to his knees, he pleaded to the heavens. "O Eternal, I do not claim innocence... but grant mercy. Deliver us!"

But the darkness offered no immediate solace. Instead, a shadow stirred—a figure not of man but of something beyond comprehension. Without warning, it lunged. Darion reacted instinctively, grappling with the being in a clash of flesh and spirit, resolve and fear. Hours passed. Sweat mingled with dust; muscles burned; lungs heaved. The stranger's strength was otherworldly, but Darion clung, driven by desperation and something deeper—*I will not let go... not until you bless me!*

And the voice came, not with anger but with a gravity that shook his core: *"What is your name?"*

"Darion," he gasped.

*"No longer. You are now **Ilyrien**—he who strives with the divine and endures. For you have wrestled with men and gods... and prevailed."*

Pain seared as his hip wrenched, yet warmth—radiant and overwhelming—flooded him. The figure vanished like mist under dawn's gaze, leaving Darion—now Ilyrien—battered but transformed.

Morning brought both fear and hope. Limping but resolved, he arranged his caravan: gifts prepared—flocks, herds, treasures—to appease Kaelen. *Let peace be bought if it cannot be won.*

Then the moment arrived. Across the plain, Kaelen and his men rode forth. Darion, bowing low seven times, awaited judgment. Yet as Kaelen drew near, something broke—a dam long held. He dismounted, strides swift. Arms opened not to strike... but to embrace. Brother met brother—anger dissolved in the river of time and shared blood.

Kaelen's voice, gruff, whispered, "I have enough, brother. Let bitterness die." Tears, long denied, welled in Darion's eyes. "Then let us begin anew."

Their paths, though reconciled, would diverge. Darion journeyed onward to **Shekareth**, the sacred ground where his grandfather **Zareon** had first built an altar beneath whispering oaks. There, among stones weathered by age and faith, he knelt, raising a fresh pillar to the heavens.

"O Eternal... You have brought me home. You have turned wrath into mercy, exile into embrace. Let this land... this promise... endure."

The winds of Velithar stirred the grasses, carrying his words into the vast expanse—where stars, constant and eternal, bore witness to covenants renewed, destinies unfolding, and a family's legacy carved into the bones of the earth.

And so, Darion—now Ilyrien—stood upon promised soil. Not as the man who fled in fear, but as one tempered by trial, humbled by grace, and ready to walk the path the Eternal had etched into the fabric of the realms.

The Twelve Scions of Darion – Founders of the Tribes.

Beneath the ever-watching stars of **Velithar**, where the rivers carved ancient paths and the winds carried whispers of both past and prophecy, **Darion**—now known to many as **Ilyrien**, the one who wrestled with the divine—became the father of twelve sons. Each boy, born from his union with **Rhaelen**, **Liraen**, and their handmaidens, carried not only the blood of a patriarch but the weight of a destiny that would shape the future of the Sacred Realms.

The birth of each son was not merely a family affair—it was the forging of pillars upon which nations would stand. Like rivers branching from a single source, they would one day flow into lands distant and diverse, carving out legacies that would echo across generations. And yet, in their youth, they were simply brothers—bound by blood, divided by rivalries, ambitions, and the affections of their fathers' wives.

Darion would often gaze upon his sons with a heart both heavy and hopeful. *Twelve... as many as the stars promised to my forefather Zareon,* he mused. *Each one a spark destined to ignite realms yet unseen.*

The Twelve Sons of Darion:

1. **Ravel** – *The Firstborn of Liraen*: Strong-willed and tempestuous, Ravel bore the weight of eldest sonship with pride but wrestled with jealousy. His ambitions often clouded his

judgment, yet his bravery was undeniable—a spearhead in battle and voice among the clans. His lineage would settle lands known for warriors and iron forges, where strength was both law and legacy.

2. **Kaelen** – *Second Son*: Not to be confused with Darion's brother, this Kaelen was fierce of spirit, inheriting his namesake's boldness. With a hunter's eye and a wanderer's soul, he would lead his tribe to the dense woodlands and craggy hills, becoming guardians of the frontier realms.

3. **Thamiel** – *The Quiet Storm*: Thoughtful and reserved, Thamiel's wisdom ran deep beneath calm waters. His descendants would become renowned for their craftsmanship and knowledge, their banners flown high in cities of learning and artistry.

4. **Zevron** – *The Flame-Tongued*: Zevron's words could both inspire and inflame. A natural leader with a silver tongue and a restless heart, his tribe would carry a legacy of diplomacy and

fierce defense of their borders, known for swift blades and swifter minds.

5. **Arel** – *The Wolf's Shadow*: Arel moved like smoke—silent, observant, and striking with precision when provoked. His line would become master trackers and scouts, their territories stretching across the wilds where few dared treads.

6. **Selian** – *The Gentle Roar*: Compassionate yet unyielding when roused, Selian's descendants would become shepherds of both people and land, cultivating fertile valleys and standing as pillars of stability amid chaos.

7. **Dariel** – *The Mirror of His Father*: Bearing Darion's name in part, Dariel inherited much of his father's cunning and introspection. His tribe would become keepers of sacred rites and ancient traditions, ensuring the covenants were remembered and honored.

8. **Veyron** – *The Swift Gale*: Quick of foot and quicker of wit, Veyron's people would become messengers and merchants,

their caravans winding across the realms, their influence felt in markets and courts alike.

9. **Lioren** – *The Iron Heart*: With a stubbornness rivaling mountains, Lioren's descendants would carve strongholds into cliffs and peaks, their warriors donning armor forged in their cavernous halls.

10. **Eloren** – *The Sea's Son*: Drawn to the Vastmere's shimmering expanse, Eloren's lineage would master the seas, navigating treacherous waves and establishing ports that thrived with trade and exploration.

11. **Sareth** – *The Flame of Promise*: Bright-eyed and visionary, Sareth spoke often of futures beyond the horizon. His descendants would carry this spirit of adventure, pushing boundaries and venturing into lands unknown.

12. **Jovren** – *The Beloved*: The youngest, born to Rhaelen in Darion's later years, Jovren was cherished beyond measure. His gentle nature belied a core of iron resolve, and his tribe would

become shepherds of peace and justice, standing as mediators when wars threatened to sunder the land.

Together, these twelve scions formed the tapestry of a nation yet unborn. Their tempers clashed, their loyalties intertwined and frayed in turns, yet destiny held firm to the promise given long ago under star-kissed skies. They were more than sons—they were the roots of kingdoms, the heartbeat of prophecies whispered by the Eternal to Zareon, carried through Eryon, and now resting upon Darion's shoulders.

In quiet moments beneath the ancient oaks of **Shekareth**, Darion would kneel at the altar his grandfather once raised. *Twelve sons... twelve tribes. O Eternal, may they not stray as I once did. May their paths be lit by Your hand, their hearts steadfast.*

Above, the stars shone brightly, silent witnesses to legacies unfolding. The Sacred Realms awaited the stories yet to be written—of betrayal and brotherhood, exile and return, trials by fire and the enduring covenant that would outlast kings and kingdoms.

And thus, from Darion's loins and legacy, the tribes of the Sacred Realms would rise—destinies forged in love, strife, and the ever-watchful gaze of the Eternal.

Veils of Sorrow – The Passing of Rhaelen and Eryon.

The lands of **Velithar**, once resonant with laughter and the clamor of life, grew muted beneath skies heavy with gathering clouds. After his long journey through exile, reconciliation, and return, **Darion** found the soil of his homeland beneath his feet once more. Yet peace, that fleeting shadow, eluded him still. No sooner had he raised his tents upon the fields near **Beth'Zereth** than sorrow crept into his camp like an unseen wind, chilling every heart it touched.

Rhaelen, beloved wife and heart of his household, whose laughter had once been the song that lightened Darion's burdens, now lay pale beneath a canopy woven with dark silks. Her breath, once steady, grew shallow with the pains of childbirth—a blessing mingled with the ache of parting. Around her, the murmured prayers of handmaidens blended with the soft weeping of her children. **Jovren**, her youngest before this birth, clung to the edge of the tent, his innocent eyes wide with confusion and fear.

Darion knelt beside her, taking her hand—once strong, now fragile as wilted petals. Her gaze met his, shimmering with both love and an unspoken farewell. "You must... carry on," she whispered, voice barely audible. "For them... for the promise." Tears, unbidden, carved paths down Darion's weathered face. *How many sacrifices must this journey demand?*

Outside, the earth seemed to hold its breath as a cry—new and piercing—broke through the somber stillness. The child, red-faced and wailing, was placed in Rhaelen's arms. Her lips formed a faint smile, a final warmth illuminating her face. "**Benariel**," she murmured. "Son of my sorrow." Her fingers traced the infant's cheek before her hand fell limp.

And just like that, the light in her eyes faded—leaving behind a void no words could fill.

Darion's chest tightened as he pressed his forehead to hers. *O Eternal... why must joy be wedded to grief?* He lifted the newborn close, heart torn between the weight of loss and the fragile hope cradled in his arms. "You shall not bear the burden of sorrow," he whispered. "Your name shall be **Valeniel**—son of the right hand."

A burial was prepared beneath the ancient oaks lining the road to **Ephrathen**. Stones were laid, earth upturned, and Rhaelen—wrapped in linens woven with threads of silver—was lowered into the embrace of the land she had journeyed to alongside her husband. The gathered kin and tribes stood in solemn silence as Darion, voice thick with grief, spoke: "Here rests Rhaelen, whose love weathered exile, whose spirit never faltered. May the Eternal hold her as I once did."

The wind stirred the trees, their leaves rustling like whispered farewells. Life would go on. Yet for Darion, a part of his soul was now buried beneath the stones and soil, beside the woman who had walked beside him through deserts, valleys, and the fires of destiny.

Seasons shifted as time's relentless march continued. Joy and sorrow ebbed and flowed through Darion's camp, but another shadow crept upon the horizon—this one colder, inevitable.

Word reached him that **Eryon**, his father—the patriarch whose hands had once blessed him, whose gaze had both judged and forgiven—was nearing the end of his days. Without hesitation, Darion gathered his sons and journeyed toward **Bevrath**, the ancient homestead where the walls seemed to echo with memories of childhood and youthful mistakes.

The once vibrant patriarch now lay upon a cedar-hewn bed, breath slow as the lapping waves of a distant sea. His hair, white as mountain frost, framed a face etched with time's passage. Eyes once sharp now glimmered with a soft, fading light. At his side stood **Kaelen**, the brother once estranged, now reconciled—grief and acceptance mingling in his posture.

Darion approached, kneeling by his father's side. Eryon's lips curled into a faint smile. "You came," he rasped.

"How could I not?" Darion's voice broke. "You are... my father."

Eryon's gaze drifted over the gathered sons—his grandsons—each a legacy born of choices made, promises kept, and paths trodden under both blessing and burden. "The Eternal's covenant... it lives on," he murmured. His hand, frail yet determined, lifted to rest upon Darion's head. "Be steadfast... guide them well... the promise... must endure."

His final breath left like a breeze slipping through open fields—gentle, inevitable, profound.

They buried him in the cave of **Mach'velen**, beside his father **Zareon** and mother **Sareah**—a tomb etched into the earth where patriarchs lay in honored rest. Candles flickered, casting amber glow upon stone walls carved with the symbols of the Eternal's covenant.

Darion lingered after the mourners departed, fingers tracing the ancient runes. *From dust to dust... yet Your promises stand, Eternal One. Through sorrow, through joy—through all that lies ahead—we endure.*

Outside, the night sky stretched vast and unending, stars shimmering as silent witnesses to generations past and futures yet to be written.

And thus, with the passing of Rhaelen and Eryon, a chapter closed—but the saga of the Sacred Realms continued, its tapestry richer with threads of love, loss, and the unwavering march of destiny.

Shadows of Betrayal – The Descent of Thalen into Zephyra.

Grief, like a shadow without end, weighed heavily upon **Darion**. The loss of **Rhaelen** still gnawed at his soul, and the echoes of his father **Eryon's** final blessing reverberated through the halls of memory. Yet even as the wounds of past sorrows remained fresh, a darker storm brewed unseen, ready to sunder his heart further.

Of his twelve sons, none held a place in Darion's heart like **Thalen**, born of his beloved Rhaelen. The boy was a dreamer, his visions woven with threads of prophecy and wonder, speaking of stars bowing and fields bending. His words, though innocent, stirred envy among his elder brothers—jealousy festered like a hidden wound, fed by Darion's visible favor toward the boy. Thalen's tunic—a garment of shimmering threads dyed in hues of royal sapphire and crimson—became a symbol not of love, but of division.

The brothers' glances darkened with each passing day. *Why him?* they muttered in hushed corners. *Why should the youngest bask in father's favor while we toil in the fields unseen?*

One morning, as the winds carried the crisp scent of distant rains, Darion summoned Thalen. "Your brothers graze the flocks near the plains of **Dathmeren**," he said, voice tinged with concern. "Go, see to their well-being. Bring me word." Thalen nodded, unaware of the fate unraveling before him. His footsteps were light, heart filled with duty and love for his kin, even as clouds thickened above the Sacred Realms.

Far beyond the rolling hills, the brothers spotted Thalen's approach. The tunic—bright as the morning sun—was a beacon that ignited their simmering rage. Words, sharp and venomous, flew between them. *"Here comes the dreamer,"* **Ravel** hissed. **Zevron** spat,

"Let us silence his visions. We'll cast him into the depths—say a beast devoured him. Then we shall see what becomes of his dreams!" Lioren, his face torn between anger and guilt, murmured, "Let us not shed blood... there are other ways."

Their schemes twisted like smoke in the air. By the time Thalen arrived, greeting them with warmth, the trap had already been set. Rough hands seized him, his confusion turning to terror. "Brothers, why—what is this?" His words fell on hearts hardened by envy. They stripped him of his tunic, casting it aside like refuse. Tears sprang to his eyes, not from the bruises inflicted, but from betrayal far deeper than flesh. "You are my brothers…" he gasped.

Without further word, they dragged him to a dry ravine—a pit carved by ancient floods—and cast him into its depths. Darkness swallowed him. Up above, voices debated, guilt warring with malice.

As fate would have it, the sound of caravan bells drifted across the wind. A procession of traders from **Kedareth**, bound for the distant sands of **Zephyra**, crested the horizon with camels laden in spices, silver, and wares. Zevron's eyes gleamed with opportunity. *"Why slay* *him? Let's sell him. Profit is better than guilt."* Agreement spread like wildfire. Thalen, hoisted from the pit, pleaded with tear-streaked cheeks, "Please... do not do this."

But silver coins clinked in eager hands, and hearts turned cold. Bound in iron chains, Thalen was led away, his gaze never leaving the horizon where his home lay hidden. His cries, swallowed by the distance, echoed through the hills long after the caravan disappeared into the Vastmere's shimmering heat.

Back at the encampment, deception wove its web. The brothers, their hands stained not with blood but with betrayal, took Thalen's tunic—soaked it in the blood of a slaughtered beast—and carried it to their father. Darion, seated beneath the ancient oak, stood as they approached. His gaze, hopeful, shattered when the garment was unfurled before him.

"We found this," Ravel spoke, feigning grief. "Is this... your son's?"

Darion's world crumbled. His hands trembled as he clutched the bloodied fabric, the colors of joy now a tapestry of sorrow. "No... no!"

His knees buckled, cries tearing from his throat. "My son... my Thalen is devoured!" Grief consumed him, fierce and unrelenting. He tore his garments, ashes cast upon his head, voice rising in lament that stirred even the coldest hearts.

No comfort could reach him. His sons, feigning sorrow, placed hands upon his shoulders—but he shrugged them off. "Leave me! I shall mourn until I descend to the depths where he now dwells!" Days turned to weeks, yet his lament never ceased. Rhaelen's loss was profound—but this... this was a wound without healing.

And far to the south, beyond the deserts that seemed to stretch into eternity, Thalen—chained and weary—arrived at the gates of **Solkaris**, the heart of **Zephyra**. Towers of alabaster gleamed beneath the relentless sun, and the streets thrummed with the cries of merchants and the clang of bronze blades. Sold like a trinket, he found himself in the household of **Pothefar**, captain of Zephyra's guard—a man whose gaze weighed every soul brought before him.

Thalen's journey of despair had only just begun. Yet, even in chains, his spirit whispered the echoes of distant dreams—the stars still spoke, the Eternal's hand unseen but ever-present. His destiny was not to wither in the sands but to rise amidst them... though the path ahead would be forged through betrayal, slavery, and the fires of trial.

Thus, the tapestry of fate stretched taut: a father drowned in grief, brothers ensnared by guilt, and a son—lost to the world—walking the road that would one day shift the course of the Sacred Realms. The stars above watched, silent sentinels to a saga unfolding beyond mortal comprehension. For in the darkest valleys, the Eternal's plan moved still, unseen... but never absent.

The Gathering of Stars – Reunion in the Realm of Zephyra.

Time, like an unyielding river, pressed onward. Across the lands of **Velithar**, skies darkened not with storm clouds but with the specter of famine. Crops withered beneath relentless suns, fields turned to dust, and rivers shrank into parched beds. Hunger gripped the Sacred Realms with iron claws, sending merchants, wanderers, and kings alike into desperation. Whispers spoke of a land to the south—**Zephyra**, the realm of eternal sands—where granaries overflowed, and bread was not a forgotten dream, but a reality guarded by the mighty.

In that land, beneath the gilded towers of **Solkaris**, sat a man robed in the finest silks, adorned with the signet of Zephyra's throne. His name upon foreign tongues was spoken with reverence and awe: **Thalen, Lord of Stores, Keeper of Life**. But beyond the titles and jeweled circlet, beneath the layers of authority and command, remained the heart of a son—scarred by betrayal, yet unwavering in the faith of visions once dreamt beneath northern skies.

Seven years of plenty had been gathered like treasures beneath the sands, stored in colossal vaults carved into the rock and guarded by soldiers clad in bronze. Now, as famine gnawed at the world, the vaults opened under Thalen's command. Bread flowed like rivers to the desperate masses. Yet among the countless faces that bowed before him, there appeared one day a group that froze his breath and sent his heart spiraling into chaos.

They came draped in travel-worn cloaks, faces haggard from the journey—**his brothers**. The same who had cast him into darkness now knelt before him, unknowing that the boy they sold was the man before them. Anger surged—then sorrow. Would vengeance be his? Or mercy? The Eternal's whispers stirred within him. The path forward was not one of wrath, but redemption.

Tests were woven like threads in a loom—probing their hearts, drawing forth repentance. And when at last the truth unfurled like dawn breaking through night, Thalen wept. *"I am Thalen,"* he revealed, voice breaking like a dam holding back tides of emotion. Shock and fear carved lines into his brothers' faces, but he stepped forward, arms outstretched. *"What you meant for ruin, the Eternal has wrought for salvation."*

Yet the circle was incomplete. One heart still beat far to the north, its pulse weighed with grief unhealed—**Darion**.

Back in Velithar, famine's shadow had stretched long and merciless. Darion, his body aged and spirit wearied, had resigned himself to mourning that seemed destined to be his final companion. Yet, when the news reached him—that Thalen lived, not in chains, but in Zephyra's highest courts—his knees gave way beneath the weight of hope rekindled. *Could it be?* Was the boy he had mourned, whose name he had uttered in countless laments, truly alive?

Thalen's invitation came with royal seal and promise of sanctuary. "Come," it urged, "for there is no need to starve when life awaits." Darion gathered his household—a caravan of sons, daughters, grandchildren—numbering seventy souls. Camels burdened with what possessions famine hadn't devoured, carts creaked beneath supplies, and children clutched their elders' hands as they journeyed toward the southern horizon. Deserts stretched vast and unforgiving, but hope lit every step.

The journey was grueling—sands burning by day, chilling by night. Yet as the towers of Solkaris rose from the dunes like spears against the sky, Darion's heartbeat quickened. He had left Velithar old and broken; he now approached Zephyra with trembling anticipation.

In the grand hall adorned with alabaster columns and banners of royal crimson, Thalen stood at the head of the court, flanked by guards and courtiers. He wore garments of Zephyrian nobility, but his eyes—those eyes—were the same that had once gazed up at Darion with youthful wonder. Silence gripped the chamber as the aged patriarch approached.

Darion's gaze locked onto Thalen's, disbelief and yearning wrestling within him. "My son," he whispered, voice cracking like dry earth. Tears blurred his vision. "I... thought you lost."

Thalen stepped forward, arms enfolding his father with the warmth of a thousand forgotten embraces. "No longer, Father," he murmured. "No longer."

Around them, siblings watched in silence—guilt, joy, and awe mingling in their hearts. Courtiers bowed their heads in respect as emotion flooded the room with a sanctity beyond royal decree.

Under Thalen's protection, the family was granted fertile lands in **Gosmereth**, a lush expanse within Zephyra's borders. Tents rose, flocks flourished, and laughter—long absent—returned to Darion's campfires. For seventeen years, Darion dwelt in this newfound peace, surrounded by children's laughter, the warmth of reunited kin, and the abiding presence of the son once thought lost to darkness.

In quiet moments, he would sit beneath palm trees swaying gently in Zephyra's breeze, gaze lifting to the starlit sky. *So many nights spent cursing the darkness,* he thought, *never knowing the Eternal's hand guided even my deepest grief.* Thalen often joined him, their silences speaking louder than words—father and son, grief healed by grace, wounds mended by time and providence.

And thus, in the twilight of his life, Darion beheld what few men live to see: sorrow turned to joy, loss transmuted into redemption. The sands of Zephyra bore the footprints of his family's survival—his lineage secure, the promise carried forth.

The journey had been long. The price, steep. But the Eternal's word endured, woven through every tear, every exile, every embrace restored.

And above, the stars glimmered—the same stars once promised to Zareon. A covenant fulfilled. A family preserved. A saga far from over.

Chapter 4

Thalen, Redeemer of the Realms

In the chronicles of the Sacred Realms, where destinies are forged by choice and consequence, few souls shine with a brilliance unmarred by shadow. Among kings and prophets, warriors and wanderers, one name echoes with unparalleled reverence—**Thalen**. He was a dreamer whose visions stretched beyond mortal understanding, a man whose journey carved a path through betrayal, slavery, power, and redemption.

Unlike the turbulent hearts of his forebears, Thalen's spirit remained untainted by the corruption that claimed many. Betrayed by blood, cast into the abyss of despair, and thrust into the fires of foreign lands, he emerged not with vengeance but with unwavering grace. His trials were many: the chains of servitude, the false accusations that sought to break him, the temptation of power's intoxicating grasp. Yet through every tempest, he walked in integrity—each hardship refining his character rather than corrupting it.

While others sought glory through conquest or cunning, Thalen's greatness was revealed in humility, wisdom, and an unshakable trust in the Eternal's design. Where lesser men would have crumbled under the weight of treachery, he stood steadfast. Where bitterness could have taken root, he extended forgiveness like a river cleansing the land.

And so, it was through this man—sold as a slave, imprisoned unjustly, and exalted to rule beneath Zephyra's throne—that the Eternal's plan unfolded. In famine's cruel grip, when death's shadow loomed over the Sacred Realms, salvation flowed from Thalen's hands.

Grain-filled storehouses replaced empty fields; mercy replaced wrath. His was not merely a political ascent—it was the rising of a redeemer whose wisdom preserved nations, whose compassion reconciled kin long divided.

This chapter unfolds the saga of a man whose journey was as treacherous as it was transformative. From the depths of betrayal to the heights of authority, from sorrow's valley to the embrace of a father thought forever lost, Thalen's story is not one of fleeting fortune but of a destiny forged by faith, perseverance, and the Eternal's unfailing purpose.

As the Sacred Realms held their breath and kings bowed in awe, one truth burned brighter than any crown: **Thalen, the Redeemer of the Realms**, was not elevated by chance—but by providence. His tale, etched in the annals of history, stands as a testament to the power of unwavering righteousness and the redemptive arc that can emerge from even the darkest beginnings.

The sands of Zephyra remember. The stars above bear witness. And the Sacred Realms shall never forget the dreamer who saved them all.

Visions of Ascendancy and Shadows of Betrayal.

Within the rolling highlands of **Velithar**, where olive groves stretched across sun-kissed hills and shepherds' songs echoed beneath the vaulted heavens, the household of **Darion** flourished with abundance and legacy. Yet beneath the surface of prosperity stirred a growing storm—one born not of enemies beyond the gates, but of discord within.

Among Darion's twelve sons, none shone brighter in his eyes than **Thalen**, child of his beloved Rhaelen. It was no mere favoritism of blood but of character—the boy's heart, unspoiled by greed or deceit, carried a purity that seemed rare even among the righteous. To honor him, Darion bestowed a tunic upon Thalen, crafted from the finest silks and dyed in hues of twilight indigo, emerald, and scarlet—a robe that flowed like a river of light when caught by the sun's embrace. Each thread whispered of distinction; every gaze upon it recognized what was unspoken—*this is the son upon whom Darion's favor rests.*

But what was a father's blessing to Thalen became a wound in his brothers' hearts. Resentment, subtle at first, festered with every glance toward that radiant robe. *Why should he be exalted above us? Do our hands not bleed for these flocks? Are our burdens not heavier?* Such whispers laced their conversations, and envy—like a slow poison—seeped deep into their souls.

Thalen, innocent to the shadows encircling him, was not silent about the visions that stirred in his sleep. For in the realm of dreams, where the veil between worlds thins and fate's tapestry is glimpsed, he beheld images strange and wondrous. One morning, beneath the golden blush of dawn, he gathered his brothers by the grazing fields and spoke with the enthusiasm of youth untouched by guile.

"Listen! Last night I dreamt: We were binding sheaves in the field, and behold—my sheaf stood upright, while yours gathered around and bowed low before mine."

Silence. Then laughter—sharp, cold. **Ravel**, ever quick with venom, sneered, "So you fancy yourself a king now, little dreamer? Shall we grovel at your feet next?" **Zevron**'s eyes narrowed, hands clenched white-knuckled. Even **Lioren**, whose heart harbored occasional pity, looked away, jaw tight with simmering frustration. Thalen's smile faltered, confusion knitting his brow. *Was it not merely a dream? Why should truth spoken breed such ire?*

Days passed, yet tension only thickened like gathering storm clouds. Then came another vision—this one even more audacious. He stood once more among them, tunic shimmering in the midday light. "Brothers," he began, voice tinged with wonder, "I dreamt again: The sun, the moon, and eleven stars... they bowed before me."

This time, anger ignited like dry tinder to flame. Zevron advanced, voice a snarl, "You dare claim the heavens themselves yield to you?" Murmurs of *arrogance... insolence* rippled through the ranks of his siblings. And when Darion, upon hearing of the dream, rebuked him with tempered words—*"Shall your mother and I, along with your brothers, indeed bow to you?"*—even then, a glimmer of contemplation danced behind the patriarch's eyes. *Could there be more to these visions than mere fancy?*

Yet for his brothers, doubt found no foothold—only envy's consuming blaze. What had begun as mild resentment now burned into hatred. Words once held back spilled forth in bitter jest. Eyes that once looked upon Thalen with brotherhood now glared with thinly veiled contempt. The tunic—symbol of favor—became a daily reminder of perceived injustice.

And as jealousy reached its peak, dark plots began to stir in hushed corners of campfires and shadowed fields. *He must be silenced,* whispered hearts darkened by bitterness. *His dreams—his favor—they must end.*

Unbeknownst to Thalen, whose nights still brimmed with celestial visions and whose days remained filled with simple kindness, the threads of betrayal wove tightly around him. Destiny's loom worked without pause, setting the stage for a fall that would pierce deeper than any blade—for betrayal by blood is the sharpest wound of all.

And so, beneath the vast expanse of the Sacred Realms—where stars watched with silent knowing—the dreamer walked toward a fate both harrowing and divine. Dreams had been spoken. Envy had been kindled. And soon... betrayal would strike.

The Pit and the Price – Descent into Darkness.

The sun blazed mercilessly over the plains of **Velithar**, casting long shadows that seemed to stretch like grasping fingers across the rugged terrain. Thalen, draped in his vibrant tunic—a cascade of colors shimmering against the arid landscape—approached the fields where his brothers tended the flocks. His steps were light, heart warmed by thoughts of family reunion, unaware that bitterness had fermented into something far darker in the hearts he sought to greet.

From a distance, the brothers saw the telltale glimmer of that tunic—*that accursed robe*, the symbol of all they resented. Zevron's jaw tightened, fists clenched until knuckles blanched. Ravel spat upon the ground, voice a venomous hiss: "Here comes the dreamer... come to lord his visions over us once more." His words, like flint striking steel, ignited their simmering rage.

Lioren's gaze wavered, uncertainty flickering—but Zevron's hand gripped his shoulder, anchoring him to resolve twisted by envy. *Enough.* The time for whispers had ended; action beckoned like a predator's hunger.

"What say you," Ravel sneered, glancing at the others, "if we silence his dreams... forever?" Silence, heavy and pregnant with grim contemplation, enveloped them until Zevron spoke—his voice cold as the northern winds, "Let us strike him down. No more visions. No more favoritism."

Yet amid the swelling darkness, **Reuven**—firstborn though not faultless—felt hesitation claw at his conscience. *Murder? Blood spilled upon our hands?* He stepped forward, voice strained, "Shed no blood. Cast him into the pit yonder. Let the wilderness claim him." His words, a compromise between wrath and guilt, found twisted acceptance. Death by their hands was avoided—*but death, nonetheless.*

Oblivious to the venom lacing the air, Thalen drew near, smile unfurling like morning's first light. "Brothers!" he called, joy untouched by suspicion. But warmth met walls of cold glares. Hands that once clasped his in youthful games now seized him with iron grips. Confusion gave way to alarm, then fear. "Wait—what are you—?" His words strangled as they tore the tunic from his body—the garment his father's love had woven now dragged through dust and disdain.

Lioren looked away, unable to meet his younger brother's pleading gaze. Zevron and Ravel did not flinch as they dragged Thalen toward the jagged maw of an ancient cistern—dark, deep, a gaping abyss in the earth. Thalen's protests echoed into futility as they hurled him downward. Rocks scraped his skin; the world spun—a kaleidoscope of sky, earth, and betrayal—before darkness swallowed him whole. His cry reverberated up the stone walls, haunting and raw, clawing at whatever shred of compassion might remain above.

Heart pounding, breath ragged, Thalen lay bruised and disoriented at the pit's bottom. *Why...?* His mind reeled. Brothers— family—had become his captors. The ground beneath him, cold and unyielding, mirrored the hearts that had thrown him there. Up above, the world continued without him. Laughter—cruel, hollow—drifted down. Overhead, the brothers sat eating bread, indifferent to his plight. The sun's glare blurred into a haze, but overhead, he caught Lioren's gaze peering down—a flicker of guilt before it vanished like a passing shadow.

Then—hoofbeats. Dust curled into the sky as a caravan emerged—a procession of **Midianite traders**, cloaked in desert garb, camels burdened with spices, balm, and wealth-seeking goods. Zevron's eyes gleamed, a darker thought unfurling. "Why leave him to die when coin can be gained?" he murmured. Agreement rippled through the brothers. *Betrayal was grim—but betrayal bought with silver was profitable.*

Bartering was swift and heartless. Thalen, pulled from the pit, stood swaying, dirt-streaked and bloodied. His lips parted in disbelief as ropes coiled around his wrists. "Please—brothers—don't do this—" His voice cracked; desperation raw. But Zevron's gaze held no mercy;

Ravel's smile twisted. "Perhaps your dreams will fare better in chains," came the cruel retort.

Thirty silver pieces exchanged hands—glinting like cold fragments of a broken bond. Thalen's eyes darted to Lioren— *please...*—but the older brother looked away, shame sealing his lips. Shoved toward the caravan, Thalen stumbled. Rope bit into flesh; foreign tongues barked orders. Every step away from the familiar fields was a severing—a cutting away of family, home, and hope.

Above, the brothers watched the caravan's silhouette shrink against the horizon. The tunic of many colors, stained with dust and smeared with lamb's blood, lay abandoned—mockery of innocence lost. Reuven's stomach twisted in regret, but words unsaid could not undo deeds done.

The caravan pressed southward. Sands shifted beneath trudging feet, and Thalen—once favored son—now bore the chains of betrayal. Tears stung but would not fall. *Why, Eternal One?* His silent plea stretched toward uncaring skies. *Why show me stars bowing if my path leads to darkness?*

Beyond the dunes awaited **Zephyra**, land of sun-scorched palaces and shadowed intrigues. There, in the city of **Solkaris**, he would be sold as property—his name bartered, his freedom stripped. And yet... beyond human schemes, the Eternal's design moved unseen.

Dreams had not lied. They simply required the journey through shadow before the rise to light.

But for now, the road stretched endless, and Thalen's steps—bound in chains—echoed toward an unknown destiny.

Appointed Governor of Zephyra

In the heart of Solkaris—the radiant capital of Zephyra—marble towers stretched toward the heavens, their alabaster walls gleaming beneath the merciless sun. The streets below pulsed with life, churning with merchants from distant lands, warriors in gleaming bronze, and priests chanting prayers to false gods whose statues loomed over the marketplaces. Yet within the grandeur of the palace, a darkness weighed upon the throne itself—one that no gold nor offering could dispel.

King Morvah, sovereign ruler of Zephyra, sat restless upon his obsidian throne, his regal robes adorned with intricate patterns of serpents and suns. His eyes, sharp as forged steel, revealed a man troubled beyond the reach of earthly counsel. Night after night, visions tormented his sleep—visions that clawed at the edges of his sanity. Seven sleek, fattened beasts grazing along the banks of the mighty River Saryndor were swallowed whole by seven gaunt, hollow-eyed creatures. Again, his dreams twisted into another vision—seven plump ears of golden grain consumed by withered stalks, blackened and wind-worn. Neither the seers nor the magi of Zephyra could unravel the enigma, their tongues quick with flattery but void of wisdom.

Whispers soon reached the ears of Pothefar, captain of the royal guard—the very man who had once claimed Thalen as a household servant. Beside him stood his cupbearer, whose own life had once teetered on the edge of execution until Thalen's interpretations of his past dreams had proven true.

"Majesty," the cupbearer ventured, bowing low, "there is a man—Thalen of Velithar—whom the Eternal has graced with insight beyond mortal ken. While imprisoned, he spoke of dreams, and what he foretold unfolded precisely as spoken."

King Morvah's gaze sharpened. "Bring him. Now."

The palace gates swung wide, and soldiers clad in scaled armor hastened to the dungeons beneath Solkaris. There, where darkness and damp air suffocated hope, Thalen knelt in silent prayer. His chains clinked softly, the iron biting into his wrists—but his spirit remained unbowed. The clamor of approaching guards shattered the gloom, and without ceremony, he was hauled to his feet.

"Come, dreamer," one guard sneered, though unease flickered in his eyes. "The king commands your presence. Mind your tongue lest your head part ways with your shoulders."

Bathed, shaven, and clothed in fresh garments of fine linen—a stark contrast to the filth-stained rags he had worn—Thalen was led through towering halls adorned with murals depicting Zephyra's conquests and gods who gazed down with indifferent eyes. Yet

Thalen's gaze did not falter; his heart anchored not in fear of earthly kings but in the Eternal's unseen hand guiding every step.

Before the throne, he knelt, the polished floor cold beneath him.

Morvah's voice cut through the hall, regal and commanding. "I have dreamed dreams that torment my soul, and none can unravel them. I hear it said you possess such skill." His gaze narrowed. "Can you interpret them?"

Thalen lifted his head, his sapphire eyes steady. "Majesty, it is not in me. But the Eternal—He who shapes the stars and commands the seas—grants wisdom beyond flesh. He shall reveal the meaning to ease your heart."

A murmur rippled through the court—such boldness before the throne of Zephyra was rare, yet Morvah, compelled by something he could not name, gestured for Thalen to proceed.

As the king recounted his visions, Thalen's expression grew solemn. Silence thickened the air, courtiers holding their breath. At last,

Thalen spoke—his voice calm yet echoing with an authority beyond mortal measure.

"Majesty, the Eternal reveals that both dreams are one and the same. Seven years of abundance shall grace Zephyra and all the Sacred Realms, the fields overflowing, the rivers generous. Yet afterward shall come seven years of famine—so grievous that memory of prosperity will wither like dust upon the wind. The doubling of the dream is certain; the matter is decreed, and swift shall its fulfillment be."

A weighty stillness followed, broken only by the faint rustle of silks as nobles shifted uneasily. Morvah's brow furrowed. "What must be done?"

"Seek out a man wise and discerning," Thalen urged, "to oversee the land. Let storehouses be filled during years of plenty, granaries overflowing as rivers in flood. Thus, when famine devours the earth, Zephyra shall stand as a sanctuary amid desolation."

Morvah sat back, eyes locked upon the young man. Whispers surrounded the throne, advisors debating in hushed tones—but the king raised a hand, silencing them all.

"Can there be found another with such wisdom?" he mused aloud. Then, louder: "Thalen of Velithar—your God's spirit rests upon you. Who better to wield this charge?" He stood, his royal mantle sweeping across the marble. "I appoint you governor over all Zephyra. None shall wield authority above you save for myself. Let this be decreed before gods and men alike."

Gasps echoed through the court, disbelief painted across the faces of nobles and generals. Yet none dared oppose the king's command.

A signet ring—heavy with gold and emblazoned with the serpent and sun crest of Zephyra—was removed from Morvah's hand and placed upon Thalen's finger. Fine robes of deep indigo and silver embroidery adorned him, and around his neck hung a chain of authority whose weight was less than the responsibility now placed upon his shoulders.

Processions paraded through Solkaris, trumpets blaring as citizens gazed upon the foreigner elevated beyond imagination. Thalen rode in a chariot of black-lacquered wood, banners streaming, his gaze distant yet resolute. Whispers filled the streets. *Who is this man that the gods favor him so?* Yet Thalen knew it was not the favor of idols but the Eternal's providence unfolding.

Years of bounty followed, as foretold. Fields swayed with golden grain, vineyards overflowed, and storehouses—constructed under Thalen's precise direction—rose like bastions against the future storm. Grain was measured, weighed, and sealed under guard, the city's granaries stretching to the horizon like a second skyline.

Then, the skies grew hard, the rains ceased, and famine—dark and merciless—descended like a shadow upon the Sacred Realms. Crops withered; rivers shrank to skeletal streams. Hunger gnawed at villages and cities alike. And from far lands, caravans laden not with goods but with desperate souls converged upon Zephyra—the only realm prepared.

Thalen stood at the gates of the storehouses, overseeing distribution with justice unyielding yet compassionate. Faces sunken with hunger bowed before him; he lifted them with kindness, ensuring none perished while stores remained. The Sacred Realms marveled—where kingdoms crumbled, Zephyra stood firm.

And so, the dreamer once cast into darkness now stood as the savior of nations. The Eternal's hand, unseen yet undeniable, had woven every betrayal and trial into this moment of providence. Yet Thalen's story was far from its final verse. Beyond the horizon, his past—marked by betrayal and the blood of brothers—would soon come to face the man he had become.

For in the Sacred Realms, destiny moves like the stars—ever turning, ever aligning with the will of the Eternal.

The Prophecy of Abundance and Desolation.

The grand hall of Solkaris fell into a heavy silence, the flickering braziers casting long shadows upon the polished obsidian floors. The assembled nobles and seers stood as still as statues, their gazes fixed upon Thalen, whose steady voice filled the chamber like a river breaking through a dam.

"The Eternal has revealed His decree," Thalen began, his words weaving through the tension-laden air, "and His hand moves swiftly across the Sacred Realms."

He paused, allowing the gravity of his pronouncement to sink into the hearts of those gathered. King Morvah leaned forward on his throne, his fingers tightening on the armrests carved with images of serpents and suns. His eyes, once clouded with confusion, now burned with a mix of fear and anticipation.

"The seven robust cows you beheld grazing beside the River Saryndor, their forms full and sleek," Thalen continued, "are the harbingers of seven years of abundance. In those years, Zephyra's fields will bloom beyond measure. The vineyards will overflow with wine, the granaries will strain beneath the weight of harvested grain, and the rivers will run generous and deep. The land itself shall sing with bounty, and every hand that sows will reap manifold rewards."

A flicker of relief passed over the courtiers, murmurs of hope stirring like the first winds before a dawn.

"But," Thalen's voice deepened, echoing through the hall like a distant storm, "the seven gaunt cows that emerged from the shadows—beasts whose ribs pierced their skin, whose hunger could not be sated—follow close behind. They signify the years that will come after seven years of famine, darker than any the realms have known. The earth will crack beneath the sun's relentless gaze, crops will wither before the harvest, and the abundance of the previous years will be devoured as if it never was."

Gasps rippled across the assembly. The seers exchanged uneasy glances, their earlier arrogance crumbling under the weight of the interpretation. Even the seasoned warriors, men unshaken by battlefields drenched in blood, paled at the thought of a famine so consuming it could erase the memory of prosperity.

Thalen's gaze swept across the hall, resting momentarily on the engraved pillars and murals depicting Zephyra's long history of conquest and wealth. "The seven thin ears of grain, scorched by the eastern winds," he continued, "mirror this truth. Plenty will give way to desolation. The harvest will fail; the storerooms will empty. Hunger will stalk the streets of Solkaris, and the lands beyond will be consumed by desperation."

His words fell like hammers upon the hearts of those present, each syllable forging the reality of what lay ahead. Yet, even as dread thickened the air, Thalen's expression did not darken with despair. Instead, his voice softened, imbued with a thread of hope.

"But this revelation is not merely a warning," he said, "it is an invitation to act. The doubling of the dream means the matter is established, and the Eternal will soon bring it to pass. Yet, in His mercy, He reveals it now so that wisdom may prevail before calamity strikes."

All eyes turned to King Morvah, who sat frozen in contemplation, the weight of his kingdom's future pressing upon his shoulders. His gaze returned to Thalen, a spark of determination igniting within his eyes. "What must be done?" he demanded, his voice cutting through the murmurs like a blade through silk.

Thalen bowed his head briefly before lifting it again. "Let Pharaoh appoint a wise and discerning man over the land of Zephyra," he said. "Let him gather and store the abundance of the coming years— grain, wine, oil—all to be guarded against the famine that will surely follow. Great storehouses must rise across the realm, and rations be measured and kept under strict watch. When the years of scarcity come, Zephyra will not only survive but stand as a sanctuary for the peoples of the realms."

King Morvah rose from his throne, his regal form casting a long shadow across the chamber. His gaze swept the hall, seeing the nodding heads of his advisors, the wary acceptance in their eyes. Turning back to Thalen, the king's voice rang out, resolute and commanding. "Can there be found another like this man, in whom the spirit of the gods— no, the Eternal—dwells?" He stepped down from the dais, his robes trailing behind him like flowing streams of molten gold. "Thalen of Velithar, your wisdom surpasses that of all my counselors. None can match the clarity with which you speak, nor the discernment you possess."

Morvah unclasped the golden ring from his own hand, its surface engraved with ancient runes and the serpent sigil of Zephyra and slid it onto Thalen's finger. "I appoint you as the regent of Zephyra," he declared. "Only my throne shall be greater than yours. You shall wield authority over all the land, answerable to none but me. Your voice will command armies, direct laborers, and shape the future of this realm."

A roar of astonishment and applause erupted throughout the hall. Courtiers, once dismissive, now bowed in reverence. Thalen stood motionless, the weight of both honor and responsibility settling upon his shoulders like an invisible mantle. His journey from the depths of despair to the heights of power was nothing less than miraculous—but he knew it was not for his sake alone. The Eternal's hand had guided him to this moment for a purpose far greater than any crown or title.

As he was draped in garments of royal indigo, embroidered with silver and scarlet threads, and adorned with a chain of office whose gleaming links felt heavier than any burden he had ever borne, Thalen's gaze turned upward. Beyond the gilded ceiling of the palace, beyond the towering spires and vast expanse of the Sacred Realms, the stars glimmered faintly in the sky—a silent reminder of dreams once dreamt and promises yet to unfold.

For in the coming years, abundance would fill the land. But Thalen's eyes saw further, beyond the feasts and full storehouses. He saw the approaching famine—a shadow lurking at the edges of prosperity—and he steeled himself for the trials yet to come.

The Eternal had spoken. The realms would heed—or perish. And Thalen, the dreamer once betrayed, now stood as the shield between life and desolation.

The Mantle of Sovereignty.

The grand chamber of Solkaris buzzed with tension as King Morvah stood before his throne, his regal figure illuminated by the flickering glow of amber lanterns and the glinting obsidian floors beneath him. Before him stood Thalen—once a foreigner, now a man whose words had pierced through the haze of confusion and dread like the morning sun breaking through storm clouds.

Courtiers, adorned in flowing robes stitched with golden filigree, whispered in hushed tones, glancing between their king and the young Velitharan. The air felt thick with anticipation; the kind that lingers just before thunder splits the sky.

King Morvah raised his hand, and the murmurs fell away like waves retreating from a shore. His gaze, sharp as a blade honed through countless wars, settled upon Thalen. "The interpretation you have given, stranger," he began, voice echoing through the chamber, "is beyond the reach of my wisest seers and dream-weavers. You have unveiled not just a warning, but a path to salvation for Zephyra." His words reverberated against the towering pillars carved with ancient symbols of serpents and suns. "It is clear the Eternal walks with you."

Turning to his council, Morvah's voice grew louder. "Who among you can match this man's wisdom? Who among you foresaw what he has revealed? Not one of you," he declared, sweeping his gaze across the hall. "Yet he stands before us with answers. Shall we ignore the gift placed before us?"

The room remained silent—awed but accepting.

Morvah descended the steps of his throne, his ceremonial robe trailing behind like a river of molten gold. Standing face-to-face with Thalen, he unclasped a signet ring from his own hand—a serpent coiled around a radiant sun engraved upon it. He extended it toward Thalen, the weight of authority gleaming beneath the torchlight. "I place my trust, and the fate of Zephyra, into your hands," he proclaimed. "From this day forth, you are Regent of Zephyra—second only to my throne. None shall lift hand or voice against you without answering to me."

Gasps echoed through the court. To raise a foreigner—an outsider—to such a position was unprecedented. Yet the weight of Thalen's words, the clarity of his visions, and the gravity of what lay ahead silenced dissent.

Thalen knelt, humility tempering the enormity of the moment. "I serve not for myself, but for the will of the Eternal and the preservation of the realms," he said, voice steady.

Morvah placed the ring upon Thalen's finger. "Then rise, Regent of Zephyra."

The royal attendants draped a mantle of deep indigo across Thalen's shoulders—its hem embroidered with threads of silver and scarlet, shimmering like the dawn's first light across the Vastmere Expanse. A golden torque was clasped around his neck, and upon his brow, a circlet of burnished bronze rested—a symbol of authority both feared and revered.

Turning to the assembly, Thalen's voice rang out with calm authority, resonating beyond the marble walls. "We have been given seven years of abundance. Let us not squander this mercy. Granaries must be constructed across the land—from the silver dunes of Aradel to the lush fields near the River Saryndor. Every sheaf of grain, every cluster of fruit, every harvest must be gathered and stored. For when the seven years of famine descend upon us like a shadow at noon, the lands beyond Zephyra will crumble... but we shall endure."

Messengers were dispatched at once, their steeds thundering across the cobblestones of Solkaris and beyond. Workers toiled under the blazing sun, erecting vast storehouses that towered like mountains across the plains. Fields flourished under Thalen's guidance, and no ear of grain went to waste. The markets buzzed with activity, carts overflowing with produce bound for the newly built silos.

Thalen rode across the kingdom, his presence commanding both respect and awe. His gaze, ever forward, never forgot the famine lurking beyond the horizon. Beneath the vibrant skies and bustling streets, he prepared for the inevitable darkness.

And King Morvah watched, pride and relief mingling in his heart. "Zephyra will stand," he murmured, "because the Eternal's hand guides us through this man."

Yet even as the storehouses swelled and the people feasted in the years of plenty, Thalen's thoughts strayed to distant lands... and distant faces. The Sacred Realms beyond Zephyra remained unaware of the storm that brewed unseen. And within Thalen's heart, beneath the mantle of power and responsibility, the whisper of his past lingered—of brothers betrayed, of a father's grief.

The sands of time slipped away. The seven years of abundance waned. And on the horizon, the famine's shadow crept ever closer, ready to test not just the resilience of Zephyra—but the soul of the Regent who now stood between life and ruin.

The Famine's Grip and the Path to Deliverance.

The years of abundance, as promised, had come and gone like the fleeting warmth of an autumn sun. Now, the Sacred Realms found themselves under a sky that seemed to bear down upon the land with relentless oppression. The rivers receded into cracked beds of dust, their once life-giving waters dwindling to bitter streams. Fields, once golden with harvest, lay barren beneath a sky devoid of mercy. A suffocating wind, carrying the scent of scorched earth, swept across the lands, whispering of hunger yet to come and sorrow yet to unfold.

In Velithar, the once fertile plains where Darion's flocks had grazed, the earth turned to iron beneath the hooves of starving livestock. Grains stored in earthen jars dwindled to crumbs, and wells—deeply dug into the heart of the land—yielded nothing but parched emptiness. Villages that once echoed with laughter now murmured with prayers and laments. Eyes turned toward the heavens, searching for rainclouds that refused to gather, for hope that seemed as distant as the stars.

Within the household of Darion, despair crept through the halls like a living shadow. His sons, once proud and strong, now wore faces etched with worry. Children's cries echoed through the night as hunger gnawed at empty bellies, and the old spoke in hushed tones of times past when the Eternal's blessings flowed like rivers—but now... now there was silence.

Darion himself, aged beyond his years by grief and hardship, sat beneath the twisted branches of an ancient sycamore, his gaze lost in the horizon's haze. Thoughts of Thalen—his beloved son, lost and mourned—haunted him still, the wound unhealed, reopened now by the relentless hand of famine. His mind battled between sorrow for what was lost and fear for what might yet be taken.

News began to spread like wildfire on the winds: beyond the Vastmere Expanse, in the distant and mystical land of Zephyra, granaries stood full to bursting, and the people there neither hungered nor thirsted. Whispers spoke of a regent—wise beyond his years—who had seen the famine's shadow long before it fell, who had prepared Zephyra's storehouses with abundance beyond measure. To the starving realms, it seemed like myth... until caravans returning from Zephyra's borders bore witness to the truth.

Summoning his sons, Darion spoke with a voice that quavered with both authority and desperation. "I have heard," he said, "that in the lands of Zephyra, there is grain... life itself. Why do you sit idle, gazing upon one another while our people perish? Go! Journey to Solkaris and bring us food, lest we and our children succumb to the dust." His words, though cracked with age, held the weight of a patriarch whose family's survival balanced on a blade's edge.

Ravel, eldest and burdened by the weight of leadership, gathered his brothers. Their eyes met—some with determination, others with hesitation—but hunger leaves little room for pride. With meager supplies and weather-worn cloaks, they set out from Velithar, their journey stretching across scorched lands and desolate valleys. The sun burned overhead, an unyielding eye watching their every step, while dust storms rose to claw at their skin and blind their path.

Days bled into nights, and their hope, though battered, clung to the promise that salvation awaited beyond the desert's cruel embrace. And finally—like a mirage solidifying into reality—the towering spires of Solkaris pierced the horizon. Zephyra's capital, a city of alabaster walls and sprawling markets, gleamed beneath the sun as if untouched by the world's suffering.

Within the city, prosperity flourished. Merchants called out to bustling crowds, fountains poured crystalline waters, and the air was thick with the scents of spices and fresh bread—a cruel contrast to the hunger that had driven Darion's sons across the wastelands. Yet their gaze turned to the grand palace where, it was said, the regent ruled with unparalleled wisdom.

Little did they know that the one who held their fate in his hands—the man whose voice could grant them life or deny them salvation—was Thalen, the brother they had betrayed and sold into chains.

Their past sins, buried beneath years of guilt and deception, were about to rise from the sands of time. For famine had driven them to Zephyra, but destiny—woven by the Eternal's unseen hand—had prepared this meeting long before hunger gnawed at their souls.

And so, with heavy hearts and empty bellies, they entered the city gates, unaware that the brother they presumed lost to slavery and dust now stood clothed in authority, watching... waiting... as the story of betrayal, redemption, and divine providence prepared to unfold before the eyes of the Sacred Realms.

Revelation and Reunion: The Unveiling of Thalen.

The towering gates of Solkaris loomed ahead, shimmering beneath the relentless Zephyrian sun. Golden banners bearing the royal seal swayed in the desert breeze, and the streets thrummed with life— merchants hawked rare spices, silks glistened under the bazaar awnings, and the air was thick with the mingling scents of incense and roasted meats. Yet, for the sons of Darion, none of this grandeur dulled the gnawing hunger in their bellies or the tension knotting their hearts.

Their journey across the Vastmere Expanse and into Zephyra had been arduous—winds biting like razors, sandstorms clawing at their cloaks, and nights spent beneath starless skies—but desperation had driven them on. Now, standing before the marble steps of the royal court, even Ravel, proud and unyielding, felt a flicker of unease. This was no common merchant's hall; it was the heart of power in Zephyra, and to seek grain meant pleading at the feet of the one who ruled it.

They were led through grand halls where alabaster columns stretched toward vaulted ceilings inlaid with sapphire and gold. Murals adorned the walls, depicting the tales of Zephyra's might and prosperity—tales now overshadowed by the famine that clawed at the surrounding realms. Servants, clad in robes of deep crimson and midnight blue, guided them to the throne room, where guards stood like statues, their spears gleaming with polished obsidian tips.

And there—seated upon an elevated dais, robed in flowing silks embroidered with symbols of the sun and moon—sat the governor of Zephyra. His face was partially veiled, but his gaze, sharp as a blade, pierced through the air with commanding presence. Thalen, unrecognizable beneath layers of regal authority and the passage of years, watched them with unreadable eyes.

Ravel and his brothers knelt, pressing foreheads to the gleaming mosaic floor. "We come from Velithar," Ravel began, voice measured but edged with urgency. "Famine ravages our land. We seek only to purchase grain, that our families may not perish."

A weighted silence stretched, broken only by the faint trickle of distant fountains. Thalen's heart pounded beneath his ornate garb. *These are my brothers.* Memories surged—laughter shared under Elyndor's trees, the sting of betrayal in their eyes as they cast him into the pit, the clinking of silver exchanged for his freedom. Yet here they knelt, unaware of the truth poised like a dagger above their heads.

"You are many," Thalen spoke at last, his voice deepened by time but steady as mountain stone. "Are you mere buyers—or spies seeking to probe the weaknesses of Zephyra?"

Gasps rippled through the brothers. Zevron's eyes flared with indignation, but Lioren's hand clamped onto his shoulder, urging silence. Ravel, suppressing bristling pride, responded, "We are sons of one man—Darion of Velithar. We have no designs against Zephyra. Hunger alone has driven us here."

Thalen's gaze flicked between them, lingering on Ravel's face—the same proud tilt of the chin he remembered—and then to Jovren, the youngest, whose eyes held a sorrowful honesty that twisted Thalen's heart. "You speak of family," Thalen murmured, "yet can such bonds endure betrayal? Can kin be trusted when greed and envy fester beneath blood ties?"

Confusion darkened the brothers' faces, but before they could speak, Thalen rose. "Leave. Return with your youngest brother you claim exists, that I might test the truth of your words." His gaze hardened. "Fail, and you shall find Zephyra's granaries closed to you."

The brothers, bewildered and troubled, obeyed. Their return journey to Velithar was filled with heavy deliberation, Ravel wrestling with the bitter demand. Yet hunger's relentless grip and their families' survival left no room for pride. Against Darion's grief-stricken protests, Jovren was sent with them back to Solkaris.

When they returned, Jovren knelt before Thalen, his gaze meeting the governors with a mixture of fear and unwavering integrity. It was then—seeing his youngest brother, innocent of past wrongs—that the wall around Thalen's heart began to crumble.

No longer able to bear the weight of concealment, Thalen dismissed his courtiers and guards. Silence fell like a blanket over the chamber. Stepping down from the dais, he reached for the veil covering his face—and slowly pulled it away.

Gasps echoed. Ravel's breath caught in his throat, and Zevron staggered back as recognition dawned like a sudden blaze. "No... it cannot be..." Arel whispered.

"It is I," Thalen said softly, voice catching with a storm of emotions. "The brother you sold—the dreamer you cast aside."

Shame, horror, and disbelief twisted across their faces. Ravel dropped to his knees. "Thalen—we... we thought you dead—"

"Dead?" Thalen's voice cracked with both sorrow and forgiveness. "Would that have eased your guilt? I was lost to you, but the Eternal's hand was upon me. Through betrayal, I found purpose. Through chains, I found freedom." His gaze softened. "Do not be distressed or angry with yourselves. It was not you who sent me here, but the Eternal's design—to preserve life, not end it."

Tears glistened in Jovren's eyes, and even Zevron's defiance dissolved into regret. Thalen, moved beyond words, embraced them— Ravel stiff at first, but then clinging to the brother he thought gone forever.

News was sent to Velithar with swiftness borne of urgency and joy: *Your son lives.* Darion, upon hearing the tidings, wept—tears of joy and sorrow intertwined. Hastily gathering his household, he embarked on the journey to Zephyra, frailty forgotten in the rush of paternal yearning.

And when father and son stood face to face beneath the Zephyrian sun, time itself seemed to hold its breath. Darion's hands weathered and trembling, cupped Thalen's face. "My son... my Thalen... is it truly you?" His voice cracked with emotion.

Thalen embraced him fiercely, tears soaking into his father's cloak. "I am here, father. I am home."

At Thalen's behest, Pharaoh of Zephyra granted them lands in the region of Goshar—fertile plains unmarred by famine—where Darion's household, numbering many, found refuge. The hunger that had driven them to foreign shores was now replaced with abundance, and the family once shattered was mended under the Eternal's providence.

Thus, through betrayal and pain, through distant lands and years lost, redemption unfolded like the petals of a flower long thought withered. The Sacred Realms bore witness to the truth: what was meant for harm, the Eternal used for good—to save many souls from perishing.

And so, beneath Zephyra's golden skies, a family was restored. The stars—those same stars Thalen once dreamed of—shone brighter that night, singing silent songs of promises kept, of destinies fulfilled, and of an Eternal hand that weaves sorrow into salvation.

The Sanctuary of Goshar.

The journey across Zephyra's vast expanse had been long, yet as Darion and his household crested the final ridge, a breathtaking sight unfolded before them—the land of Goshar. It stretched like an emerald tapestry amidst the arid sands, kissed by the rivers that wound through fertile fields. Verdant plains rolled out beneath skies painted with the hues of a descending sun, and distant groves swayed under the cool evening breeze. This was no ordinary land—it was a sanctuary, a rare jewel nestled within Zephyra's otherwise unforgiving terrain.

Word of their arrival had preceded them. Rows of Zephyrian soldiers, clad in burnished bronze and crimson cloaks, flanked the procession, guiding them through the paved roads toward the grand encampment where Pharaoh's emissaries awaited. Though adorned in splendor, the Zephyrian guards held a respectful demeanor—aware that these were not mere wanderers, but kin to Thalen, Redeemer of the Realms and the savior of Zephyra's people.

Pharaoh himself, resplendent in golden robes embroidered with sapphire threads, awaited beneath a towering pavilion draped with banners of sun and moon sigils. His headdress gleamed beneath the twilight glow, and his gaze was regal, yet tempered with warmth.

Darion, aged but dignified, stepped forward. His long journey had etched lines of weariness upon his face, but within his eyes burned the unyielding fire of a patriarch who had found his long-lost son. He knelt before Pharaoh with reverence, yet before his head could fully bow, Pharaoh gestured for him to rise.

"You are the father of Thalen," Pharaoh said, his voice resonant, carrying both command and kindness. "Through his wisdom, Zephyra has flourished amid famine. Through his hand, lives were spared, including those beyond our borders. You are welcome here, Darion of Velithar. The Eternal's favor rests upon you and your house."

Darion's heart swelled with gratitude. "May the Eternal bless your generosity, great Pharaoh. To find not only my son alive but to receive such kindness from the realm he serves... it is more than I could have hoped for."

Pharaoh's lips curved into a faint smile. "It is not kindness, but justice—and recognition of the providence that has guided these events.

Zephyra honors those whom the Eternal raises up." His gaze shifted beyond Darion to the multitude gathered—sons, daughters, servants, and flocks numbering in the hundreds. "This land of Goshar shall be yours—a place for your flocks to graze, your people to prosper. It is the most fertile land in all Zephyra, sustained by the rivers that flow from the northern highlands and the grace of the Eternal."

A murmur of relief and joy rippled through Darion's household. Children clung to their mothers with newfound hope, and shepherds gazed in awe at the sprawling pastures awaiting them. Even Ravel, whose stern countenance rarely softened, allowed himself a smile as he envisioned fertile fields stretching toward distant horizons.

Thalen stepped forward, his Zephyrian robes billowing in the warm breeze. Turning to his family, he spoke with emotion thick in his voice, "This land is not just a refuge—it is a second chance. Here, our people shall not merely survive; we shall thrive, standing as witnesses to the Eternal's mercy and providence."

As twilight deepened into night, braziers were lit along the camp's perimeter, casting golden light upon the gathering. Pharaoh dined with Darion's household under a canopy of stars, and songs of gratitude echoed across the fields—melodies both foreign and familiar blending in a harmony that transcended borders and past wounds.

Soon, tents rose across the plains of Goshar, and flocks grazed upon grass that seemed to dance beneath the moon's gaze. Streams meandered through the land, pure and life-giving, nourishing both soil and soul. The people of Darion's house labored with joyful purpose, carving out homes beneath the sheltering arms of ancient oaks and planting fields that would yield abundance in the seasons to come.

And there, amidst the flourishing land, Darion built an altar of stone. Beneath the vast expanse of the heavens, he knelt upon the earth, lifting his voice in prayer. "O Eternal, who turns sorrow to joy and exile to home... You have guided us through darkness into light, through famine into plenty. May this land be a testament to Your unfailing promise."

His voice, though carried away by the night wind, seemed to linger across the plains, weaving into the very fabric of Goshar—a land born of loss, redeemed by grace, and destined to cradle a people whose lineage would shape the destiny of realms beyond imagination.

Thus, under the watchful gaze of the stars and the blessing of Pharaoh, Darion's family found sanctuary. The land of Goshar, lush and abundant, stood as a living testament: what was once barren was now fertile, what was once broken was now whole. And amid the fertile plains, the story of a family—once fractured by jealousy and betrayal—unfolded anew, bound together by forgiveness, redemption, and the enduring hand of the Eternal.

Thalen's Final Days – The Whisper of Promised Horizons.

Time, relentless and unyielding, had traced its course across Thalen's life like the rivers that carved the lands of Zephyra. The boy who once gazed at the stars with dreams beyond comprehension had become a man whose wisdom and mercy saved realms. Decades of prosperity had passed since the famine's shadow lifted, and under his guidance, Goshar flourished, its fields golden with harvest and its rivers singing songs of abundance. Yet even in times of peace, the passing of years etched silver into Thalen's hair and carved lines of experience upon his face.

Now, at one hundred and ten winters, Thalen's breath grew slower, his steps more measured. His gaze—once alight with youthful vision—now bore the weight of a life spent in sacrifice and service. Yet, in his twilight, a deeper glow remained in his eyes—a steadfast hope not anchored to Zephyra's courts or fields but to a promise far older than his days: the covenant spoken to his forefathers, whispered by the Eternal Himself.

Word spread swiftly through Goshar: *Thalen calls for the elders.* Across the settlements, shepherds laid down their staffs, craftsmen set aside their tools, and warriors sheathed their blades. Men whose faces bore the weathered marks of labor and women whose hands had shaped homes and generations gathered in reverence. They assembled before the pavilion where Thalen rested—a structure woven with deep blue silks and banners bearing the emblem of a rising sun over the Vastmere.

Thalen reclined upon a bed of finely woven linens, his body frail but his spirit undiminished. Beside him stood Darion's surviving sons, their heads bowed in solemn respect. Jovren, now a man of resolute kindness, held his uncle's hand, while Ravel, ever the proud firstborn, stood with a shadow of sorrow clouding his fierce eyes. Around them, the elders knelt, their breaths hushed, awaiting the Redeemer of the Realms to speak.

With effort, Thalen's voice rose—gentle yet imbued with a strength that belied his frailty. "Brothers... sons of Darion... people of the Eternal's covenant," he began, his gaze sweeping the assembly. "You have seen with your own eyes how the Eternal's hand has guided us. From famine to plenty, from sorrow to joy, He has neither forgotten nor forsaken us."

A soft breeze stirred the pavilion, carrying with it the scent of blossoming myrren trees. Thalen's lips curved into a faint smile as he continued, "Yet this land... as rich and abundant as it is... is not our home." Murmurs rippled through the crowd, but his raised hand stilled them. "The Eternal promised our father Zareon—through him to Eryon, and to Darion—that we would possess a land of our own. Not as wanderers... not as guests... but as heirs. *Velithar awaits us.*"

His words struck like a bell ringing across still waters, awakening memories of distant lands and ancient promises. Some lowered their heads in contemplation; others clenched their fists with newfound resolve.

"My time draws to a close," Thalen's voice softened, but conviction burned within every syllable. "Yet I say to you, as surely as the rivers flow and the stars burn in the heavens—the Eternal will visit you. He will raise a deliverer from among you, one who will lead our people from this realm of foreign gods back to the soil promised to our fathers." His gaze found Jovren's, who nodded with misted eyes.

A moment of heavy silence followed. Then Thalen, with effort, reached beneath his cloak and produced a small, weathered scroll—its seals bearing the sigils of the ancient covenant. "Guard this... let it be a witness among you," he whispered. "When the time comes... carry my bones with you to Velithar. I will not rest here, in this land of exile."

The elders bowed low, hands pressed over their hearts, swearing silent oaths to honor his final request. Outside, the wind rose, stirring the banners until they rippled like waves upon the Vastmere.

Thalen's gaze lifted beyond the gathering, beyond the pavilion's silken canopy, to the sky ablaze with the colors of dusk. Stars began to pierce the indigo expanse—familiar sentinels that had watched over him since boyhood. *The same stars... the same promise,* he thought. His breathing slowed, yet peace washed over him.

As night descended upon Goshar, songs of remembrance echoed across the fields—melodies of gratitude, sorrow, and hope intertwined. Thalen's body grew still, his final breath a whisper upon the wind: "*He is faithful... always faithful.*"

Thus ended the days of Thalen, Redeemer of the Realms, a man whose journey from betrayal to exaltation wove through sorrow and triumph yet always returned to the steadfast promise of the Eternal. His legacy did not fade with his passing; it lived in the hearts of his people, in the land they tilled, and in the stars that guided their gaze homeward.

And so, as the Sacred Realms turned the page to another chapter, the bones of Thalen rested beneath Zephyra's sky—but not forever. For beyond the rivers, beyond the mountains, the land of promise waited. And the Eternal's word, like the stars themselves, could not be broken.

The Last Request – Bones Bound for Velithar.

As the final embers of Thalen's life flickered, his gaze—steady even in frailty—held a resolve as enduring as the mountains that cradled the Sacred Realms. His body, worn by years of trial and triumph, lay in quiet repose beneath the silken pavilion where banners fluttered gently in the twilight breeze. The elders had gathered, their faces shadowed with sorrow, yet eyes lifted in reverence for the man whose wisdom had guided them through famine and fortune.

Summoning the last of his strength, Thalen's voice rose—a mere breath upon the wind yet carrying the weight of destiny. "*Hear me... sons of Darion, children of the Covenant.*" His gaze swept across the assembly, resting upon Jovren—the beloved, steadfast and gentle—

who knelt at his side. "The Eternal has not forgotten His promise... nor must you." His breath hitched, but determination burned fierce within. "When He comes—when His hand moves to lead you from these foreign lands—*do not leave me behind.*"

His withered hand grasped Jovren's arm with surprising strength. "Swear to me... when the time comes... carry my bones from Zephyra. Let them rest not beneath these sands, but in the land sworn to our forefathers—*Velithar,* where the Eternal's breath first blessed the soil. Let my bones lie beneath the same stars that watched over Zareon... that sheltered Eryon... that cradled Darion."

Tears brimmed in Jovren's eyes, yet he bowed his head, pressing his palm to Thalen's hand. "I swear it, uncle. By the Eternal's name, I will not let you rest here forever. Your bones will journey home."

A faint smile creased Thalen's lips—peace settling over him like the dusk settling over the land. "Good... for even in death... the promise calls." His gaze turned skyward, where the first stars glistened like scattered gems upon the night's velvet shroud. His final breath, soft as a sigh, slipped away—carried by the winds toward distant horizons.

Seasons turned.

Fields that once flourished beneath Thalen's stewardship ripened and withered in their cycles. His body, preserved according to ancient rites, lay within a stone-carved sepulcher, guarded by torches whose flames flickered with the vigil of a people who remembered. Pilgrims journeyed to the tomb, laying offerings of myrrh and hyacinth, whispering prayers beneath their breath.

And the vow endured.

Through years that stretched into decades, through shifting kings and rising empires, the memory of Thalen's request was passed from tongue to tongue, father to son, like an ember sheltered against the winds of forgetfulness. "Carry him home," they would say. "Do not forget the bones of the Redeemer."

Then—*the time came.*

Whispers spread across Goshar like wildfire on dry grass. *"The Eternal moves. Deliverance draws near."* Lanterns lit the streets, caravans stirred, and hearts swelled with both trepidation and hope. And at the heart of it all stood Jovren's descendants—keepers of the oath, now ready to fulfill it.

At dawn, beneath a sky ablaze with crimson and gold, the tomb was opened. The air, heavy with incense and reverence, quivered as the stone lid was lifted. There lay Thalen's bones, bound in ceremonial linens of deep blue and silver—the colors of his house and of the covenant he upheld. Hands, trembling with awe, lifted the remains, placing them upon a crafted bier adorned with carved runes and the emblem of the rising sun.

An escort formed—warriors, priests, and children alike— forming a procession that stretched beyond sight. Songs rose on the morning wind, voices weaving together in ancient hymns that spoke of promise, faith, and the return to sacred soil. The Vastmere's waves shimmered beside them, reflecting the solemnity of their journey.

Through deserts that burned and forests that whispered forgotten tales, they marched. The stars above guided them—silent sentinels to their purpose. Nights were spent by flickering campfires, elders recounting Thalen's life, ensuring no child among them would forget the man whose dreams once seemed folly, yet whose wisdom had shaped the destiny of nations.

And at last—*Velithar.*

The soil, rich and dark, crumbled beneath their feet like an embrace. Hills rolled like gentle waves; trees stretched upward as if reaching to welcome them home. Beneath the shade of an ancient terebinth—the same under which Zareon had once raised an altar—they laid Thalen's bones to rest.

Stones were placed, not as mere markers, but as a testament. Upon the largest, an inscription glimmered in morning light:

"Here lies Thalen, Redeemer of the Realms—dreamer, servant, brother, and son of promise. From betrayal to honor, from chains to throne, his path was woven by the Eternal's hand. Though his bones rest, his legacy walks with us—toward the dawn that never fades."

And as the wind stirred the grass, carrying the scent of wildflowers and earth, it seemed the land itself exhaled—a homecoming fulfilled.

Thus was the vow kept.

Thus was Thalen's final request honored.

And as the Sacred Realms continued to turn beneath the heavens, his story—etched in earth and sky—remained a beacon for all who would walk the path of faith, endure the fires of trial, and cling to promises spoken beyond the veil of time.

The Twilight of Thalen – Gathering to the Ancestors.

The skies above Solkaris, capital of Zephyra, blazed with the hues of an amber twilight. Crimson clouds stretched like molten rivers across the horizon, casting long shadows over the alabaster towers and bustling streets. Yet within the palace halls, where banners of deep sapphire and silver hung in silent tribute, the world seemed to pause.

Word had spread across the Sacred Realms: *Thalen, Redeemer of the Realms, was nearing the end of his days.*

In the chambers perfumed with myrrh and hyacinth, the air thickened with reverence. Flickering lanterns illuminated walls carved with scenes of Thalen's journey—from the betrayal that cast him into chains to his rise as Zephyra's highest governor, savior of countless lives. Elders, warriors, priests, and kin gathered, their faces a tapestry of sorrow and gratitude.

Thalen lay upon a bed draped in silken cloth dyed in the hues of twilight. His hair, once dark as the storm-washed seas, had turned silver, shimmering like the stars that now pierced the dusk beyond the balcony. His gaze, though softened with age, still held the luminous clarity that had guided a nation through famine and turmoil.

Jovren, his beloved nephew—the one who had sworn to carry his bones to the promised lands—knelt beside him. Tears glistened in the younger man's eyes, yet Thalen's smile was serene.

"Jovren…" His voice was a whisper yet carried the weight of mountains. "The Eternal... His hand has never faltered." He paused, breath catching like the ebbing tide. "My journey... from pit to palace, from chains to crown... was never mine alone. He walked each step beside me." His eyes drifted upward, tracing the stars emerging beyond the open window. "And now... I go to where my fathers await."

His family and trusted advisors bowed their heads, lips murmuring prayers. The room seemed suspended between realms— earth and eternity drawing near.

With what strength remained, Thalen lifted a trembling hand, reaching toward the heavens. His lips formed words only the spirits beyond could fully grasp—a final prayer, a whispered gratitude. His chest rose, fell... and did not rise again.

Outside, the city bells tolled—a deep, resonant sound that echoed across the rooftops, over the markets, through the meandering streets of Solkaris. Traders paused mid-barter, warriors halted their drills, and children looked skyward, sensing a shift in the fabric of the world. The Redeemer of the Realms had passed.

His body was adorned in royal garments—robes of silver and deep blue, the sigil of Zephyra and the house of Darion embroidered over his heart. Upon his brow, a circlet of tempered steel and onyx rested—a symbol not of kingship but of wisdom and sacrifice.

By dawn, the streets of Solkaris overflowed with mourners. Warriors clad in gleaming armor formed a solemn procession; their swords inverted in tribute. Priests chanted ancient hymns, their voices weaving through the air like threads binding heaven and earth. Thalen's bier, crafted from darkwood and etched with silver runes, was lifted upon the shoulders of twelve chosen bearers—one from each tribe born of Darion's lineage.

As the procession wound through the city, petals of white and azure rained from the rooftops. The Vastmere's waves crashed against the distant shores as if bidding farewell. From Zephyra's gates to the distant roads that stretched toward Velithar, people lined the paths— heads bowed, hands pressed to hearts.

They journeyed beyond the desert sands and rolling plains, beyond the forests where ancient trees whispered of ages past. And when at last they reached the sacred grounds of Velithar—where the

Covenant of the Eternal had been spoken, where Zareon's feet had once stood—the air seemed to shimmer with an unseen warmth.

There, beneath a venerable tree whose roots drank deeply from the earth blessed by the Eternal, they lowered him into the tomb prepared alongside the bones of his forefathers. Stones, carefully carved with the chronicles of his life, were placed around the grave, forming a circle—a symbol of completion, of promises kept and journeys fulfilled.

Upon the central stone, in letters of silver inlay, the inscription read:

Here rests Thalen, Redeemer of the Realms—betrayed yet unwavering, enslaved yet triumphant, forgotten yet exalted. His dreams, once scorned, became the salvation of nations. Though his breath has ceased, his legacy sings through the winds, the waters, and the hearts of all who walk the Sacred Realms. The Eternal called, and he answered.

As the final stone was set, the people raised their voices in a song that echoed through valleys and over mountains—a song not of sorrow alone, but of hope, remembrance, and the faith that death is but another step upon the Eternal's path.

The stars above, now bright and countless, seemed to pulse with quiet approval. And as the winds swept across the land, carrying the final notes of farewell, one could almost hear—beneath the breath of the world itself—the faintest whisper: *"Well done, faithful one. Rest now and rise again in the time beyond time."*

Thus, after a long and fruitful life, Thalen was gathered to his ancestors. His bones lay at rest, but his story—etched into the very soul of the Sacred Realms—would never be forgotten.

Chapter 5

Velithar in Exile: The Twilight of Promises

The Sacred Realms, once marked by wandering patriarchs and whispered covenants, now beheld a new season—one where the descendants of Darion flourished in foreign lands. The journey that began with famine and fear had led the House of Velithar into the heart of Zephyra, the realm of golden sands and towering monuments. What was once a temporary refuge had become a cradle for generations.

Velithar's people prospered beneath the shadow of Solkaris's gleaming spires. Under Thalen's wisdom and favor with the Zephyrian throne, they had settled in the fertile lands of Goshevar—a lush expanse kissed by the waters of the Neryth River, where flocks multiplied, and fields ripened with abundant harvests. Their songs echoed through the valleys, children's laughter filled the markets, and the Eternal's promises seemed tangible, wrapped in prosperity and peace.

Yet time—ever shifting, ever relentless—would not hold still.

As the sands of years slipped through the hourglass, the name of Thalen, once a beacon of reverence, began to fade into legend. New kings rose in Zephyra—rulers who cared little for past debts or ancient covenants. Whispers turned to murmurs, and murmurs to declarations: *"These Velithari grow numerous… too strong, too proud. What if they turn against us?"* Fear—insidious and cold—crept into the hearts of Zephyra's rulers, breeding suspicion and resentment.

What had been sanctuary now teetered on the edge of oppression.

But this was not just the tale of a nation's rise or a foreign king's fear. It was the unfolding of ancient words spoken long before—promises that through Velithar, the realms would be blessed, and trials that would forge them into something greater. Darkness would gather, chains would clink in the streets of Goshevar, and cries for deliverance would pierce the heavens.

Yet in the encroaching shadow, the Eternal's hand moved still— unseen, unwavering.

For the forge of oppression would not shatter Velithar's people. It would shape them. Mold them. Prepare them for a deliverance written in the stars before the world's foundations were laid.

Thus begins the saga of **Velithar in Exile**—a chapter of hardship, of longing, of the twilight before dawn. The Sacred Realms would tremble, tyrants would rise and fall, and the hearts of a people would be tested in the fires of affliction.

And from the depths of despair... hope would awaken.

Era of Abundance: The Blessed Years of Velithar.

In the early days of their sojourn within Zephyra—the realm of endless sands and glimmering palaces—the people of Velithar flourished like a verdant oasis amidst the desert's relentless embrace. Goshevar, the fertile expanse granted to them by the Zephyrian throne, stretched far beyond what their forefathers had ever dared to imagine: a land kissed by the silver tendrils of the Neryth River, where golden fields swayed beneath azure skies and orchards bloomed with the bounty of every season.

Here, the descendants of Darion—once wanderers and sojourners—found rest. Flocks multiplied, their wool gleaming like starlight upon the hills; herds fattened upon the rich grasses, their numbers vast as the sands themselves. Vineyards sprawled across the land, heavy with fruit that glistened like amethyst and garnet beneath the sun's warmth. From sunrise to twilight, the air thrummed with life—laughter echoing from the villages, songs rising in thanksgiving to the Eternal, and the clamor of markets bustling with trade and abundance.

Velithar's people remembered the covenant. Altars of stone, carefully hewn and set upon hills, burned with offerings of gratitude. The name of the Eternal was whispered upon the wind and sung beneath the stars. Stories of Thalen—the Redeemer of the Realms—and Darion, his father, passed from elder to child, kindling the fires of hope and heritage. It was said that the very skies above Goshevar gleamed brighter, as if the Eternal's favor rested upon the land itself.

Under the canopy of peace, generations blossomed. Children danced along the banks of the Neryth, their laughter mingling with the river's gentle song. Craftsmen and artisans, emboldened by prosperity, carved intricate works from wood and stone, their creations adorning homes and sanctuaries. Shepherds sang to their flocks under twilight's glow, and farmers rejoiced as harvests overflowed beyond what storehouses could hold.

Zephyra's courts, for a time, regarded Velithar with respect. Their trade enriched the realm, their skills in metallurgy and agriculture unmatched. The land of Goshevar, once a gift, became the beating heart of Zephyra's bounty—a partnership born of necessity, yet flourishing with unexpected harmony.

For nearly a hundred years, peace reigned. The Sacred Realms looked upon Velithar's people and saw a nation transformed—

descendants of wandering patriarchs now rooted in abundance. Yet, beneath the surface of prosperity, destiny stirred. Time, ever the silent harbinger of change, crept forward with unseen purpose.

For while fields yielded abundance and hearts swelled with gratitude, the cycle of kingdoms and memories is ever fickle. The blessed years—though rich and golden—were but the calm before a gathering storm, the hush before winds of oppression would rise from the east, casting long shadows over the land of Goshevar.

But for now, the people rejoiced. The rivers sang. The fields thrived. And the Sacred Realms held their breath, awaiting what the turning of ages would bring.

The Shifting Sands of Tyranny.

The days of laughter and abundance waned like the fading glow of a dying ember. Seasons turned, and with them, the tides of fortune began to shift. The Zephyrian throne, once a seat of alliance and benevolence, was claimed by a new sovereign—a pharaoh whose gaze upon the people of Velithar was one of suspicion, not favor. His name was whispered among the common folk, his presence heralded by the clang of bronze and banners that rippled like ominous clouds sweeping across the desert.

Where once the halls of Solkaris welcomed the leaders of Velithar with open arms, now those gilded gates closed like the jaws of a predator. The pharaoh, ensnared by fear and pride, sat upon his alabaster throne and beheld the swelling multitudes of Velithar with dread. *"Look,"* he spoke before his council, his voice a serpentine hiss that slithered through the marble chamber, *"the people of Velithar grow vast, their numbers like the stars—uncountable. If war should arise, what prevents them from siding with our enemies? Shall we let them dwell in our land unchecked, only to rise against us when our backs are turned?"*

His words ignited the kindling of fear. Courtiers nodded; voices joined in grim agreement. Thus, was birthed a decree that would bleed the joy from Goshevar and drown its fields in sorrow.

What began as subtle encroachments became overt acts of subjugation. Taskmasters emerged—men clad in iron and wielding whips braided from serpent leather—marching through villages with eyes as cold as Zephyra's deepest tombs. *"By the pharaoh's command,"* they barked, *"Velithar's hands shall build the empire they leech from!"*

Fields once lush and alive with harvest songs now echoed with the clang of forced labor. Men and women, their backs bent beneath burdens heavier than stone, toiled beneath a sun that scorched without mercy. Brick kilns, monstrous furnaces that belched black smoke, devoured countless hours of sweat and blood. Clay-stained hands molded bricks, while overseers cracked whips that sang songs of pain through the air. Crops were no longer gathered for Velithar's tables but seized to fill the coffers of Solkaris.

The Neryth River, once a source of life and laughter, ran red at dusk with the dust of their labors. Children cried for fathers too weary to lift their heads. Elders who had once told stories of Darion's journey and Thalen's redemption now sat in silence, their eyes hollow, watching as generations were shackled not by iron alone, but by despair.

The oppression deepened. Pharaoh's fear festered into cruelty, and whispers of a darker decree sent chills through every hearth: *"Their numbers must be controlled,"* the sovereign snarled. *"Their strength, broken before it becomes our undoing."*

And so, in shadowed corners, plans were forged to snuff out hope itself. Midwives were summoned, and dark commands were issued—commands that would soon stain the streets with silent grief and drown lullabies in sorrow.

Goshevar's skies, once painted in hues of gold and sapphire, seemed perpetually gray. Yet amidst the darkness, glimmers of defiance flickered in the eyes of a few. Songs of old, once joyous, became murmured prayers beneath breath—*"O Eternal One, hear us... rescue us from this affliction."*

The Sacred Realms watched in silence as the sands shifted from blessing to bondage. The cries of Velithar ascended like smoke toward the heavens, carried by winds that whispered of ancient promises yet unfulfilled.

For though darkness reigned, and tyranny's grip tightened, destiny stirred beneath the surface. The Eternal, ever watchful, heard the cries echoing from the land of chains. And even as the people's hope withered like flowers beneath a merciless sun, the seeds of deliverance had already been planted—hidden in the shadows of oppression, awaiting their appointed hour to bloom.

Chains of Stone and Shadow.

With fear gnawing at his pride, the pharaoh of Zephyra's gleaming throne halls resolved to crush the spirit of Velithar beneath the weight of servitude. No longer would the children of Velithar roam freely across the fertile plains of Goshevar; no longer would their voices echo with laughter beneath the sun-dappled groves. In his twisted vision, he sought to reduce them to nothing more than shadows, their identities buried beneath the dust of labor and the lash of whips.

"Make them bend. Make them break. Let their bodies fuel the rise of Zephyra's glory," came the tyrant's decree.

Thus began the darkest chapter in the lives of Velithar's people. Armed overseers, clad in armor etched with the serpent sigil of Zephyra, descended upon Goshevar like a storm cloud ready to consume all in its path. Fathers were torn from their homes, sons dragged from the embrace of mothers whose wails filled the valleys like a mournful dirge. Even the elderly, whose bones ached with age, were given no respite. None were spared the yoke of oppression.

The fields that once sang with harvest now bore the groans of forced labor. Under a sun that seemed to burn with newfound cruelty, the people of Velithar were driven to toil beyond the limits of mortal endurance. Their bare hands, bloodied and cracked, stacked stone upon stone for monuments that would never bear their names. Cities of grandeur—Solkaris's twin fortresses of *Merukath* and *Varneth*—rose from the sands on the backs of slaves whose names the Zephyrian lords deemed unworthy to remember.

Massive stone blocks, hauled by ropes that tore flesh and sinew, creaked across the desert plains. Each pull of the ropes brought cries of agony, yet any pause was met with the lash—a cruel serpent's kiss that left scars both visible and unseen. The whips, barbed with obsidian shards, painted backs with crimson stripes, while the taskmasters jeered with voices dripping venom. *"Faster, wretches! These walls shall outlast your miserable lives!"*

The construction of temples to false gods consumed countless lives. Towering ziggurats clawed at the skies, casting long shadows over quarries stained with sweat and sacrifice. The Eternal One's name was spoken only in hushed prayers between gasping breaths, as the people dared to hope that their cries would pierce the heavens.

Children, too young to bear burdens, were conscripted as water bearers, stumbling across the dust-choked fields with jars too heavy for their small frames. Many collapsed beneath the weight, their tears mingling with the dust as they were dragged away, replaced without thought or mercy.

Nightfall brought no relief—only darkness under which the people collapsed into restless slumber upon cold, unyielding ground. Dreams offered no solace; they were haunted by the crack of whips, the barked commands of overseers, and the ever-growing despair that they might never see freedom again. Mothers whispered lullabies not of peace, but of survival—soft words of endurance beneath a canopy of stars that seemed to flicker with distant sorrow.

Yet amidst the oppression, a stubborn ember refused to die. Old men recounted the stories of Darion, Thalen, and Vaelen—heroes whose names stirred something fierce in the hearts of the broken. *"The Eternal does not forget,"* they whispered in secret gatherings. *"He sees beyond these walls of stone and hears what kings choose to ignore."*

But the pharaoh, drunk on power, pressed harder. *"They thrive still? Increase their burdens! Break their bodies until even hope flees from them!"* New decrees echoed through the land: double the labor, halve the rations. Build faster. Build higher. Build or die.

And so, the people of Velithar labored beneath a sky that seemed to weep for them, constructing wonders of stone that gleamed like jewels against the desert backdrop—monuments to vanity and tyranny, built with the bones of the oppressed. But beyond the reach of whips and the gaze of cruel masters, a truth stirred like a whisper carried on the desert winds:

Chains may shackle the body, but they cannot bind destiny.

Even as the walls of Zephyra's pride rose higher, so too did the cries of the enslaved ascend, weaving through the clouds and into the halls of the Eternal. And in that celestial realm, unseen by mortal eyes, the first stirrings of deliverance began to move—subtle, inevitable, and soon to sweep across the Sacred Realms like a storm no pharaoh could halt.

The Flourishing Amidst Chains.

Despite the cruel yoke of Zephyra's oppression, an extraordinary phenomenon unfolded within the Sacred Realms—a growth so remarkable it defied mortal understanding. Under the searing gaze of the sun and the relentless crack of the whip, the people of

Velithar multiplied like rivers swelling with rain. No burden could break their lineage, no decree halts their increase. Where oppression sought to suffocate, life flourished with astonishing tenacity.

What began with seventy souls—descendants of Darion and his sons—soon surged into multitudes, sprawling across the valley of Goshevar. Children were born with cries that pierced the dawn, their voices a defiance against the darkness pressing upon their people. Mothers cradled infants with fierce tenderness, whispering blessings beneath the gaze of cold-hearted overseers. Fathers, though bent beneath the weight of stone and lash, found fleeting moments to teach their young sons how to endure, how to stand, how to hope.

The lands of Goshevar, though overshadowed by Zephyra's tyranny, were fertile and rich, nourished by the rivers that wound through the valley like veins of silver. Grain fields ripened beneath golden skies, and orchards bore fruit that sustained not only bodies but spirits. The Eternal's unseen hand provided sustenance, for even the hardest labor could not deplete what the earth—by divine mercy— yielded to His people.

And so, the clans expanded. Tribes once small now stretched across the land like the spreading branches of ancient trees, their roots deep and unyielding. Banners of the twelve houses—each bearing symbols of their ancestral forefathers—fluttered in hidden corners, reminders of a heritage that could not be erased. Children learned the names of their forebears: Ravel the strong, Zevron the eloquent, Arel the shadowed tracker, Sareth the flame of promise. Legends were passed around flickering fires after long days of toil, tales that kindled identity amidst slavery.

Despite the increasing cruelty of Zephyra's rulers, the numbers of Velithar swelled beyond measure. The cries of newborns echoed from one horizon to another, defying the pharaoh's fears. With every child born, dread grew in the heart of Zephyra's court. *"How do they thrive beneath our boot?"* the nobles whispered. *"We burden them beyond breaking, yet they multiply like stars in the night sky."*

In the royal halls of Solkaris, councillors spoke in hushed urgency. *"Should war come, they will stand as a nation within our walls—an army from within!"* Their dread was not unfounded, for of the millions now dwelling in Goshevar's lands, six hundred thousand were men of fighting age—warriors whose strength had been forged under oppression, whose backs could carry the weight of nations, and whose hearts, though wearied, smoldered with the embers of resolve.

The growth was not mere chance, nor simply the blessing of fertile land and nourishing harvests. It was the undeniable mercy of the Eternal, whose covenant with Zareon and his descendants burned brighter with every passing generation. Even in the shadow of tyranny, He preserved His people—sheltering them like seeds buried beneath winter's frost, destined to break forth when the season of deliverance arrived.

What had begun with a family had become a multitude—a people vast as the sands of the Vastmere's shores, numerous as the stars that spanned the Sacred Realms' skies. Pharaoh's dread deepened with every census, his heart twisting with fear and pride, but the people of Velithar held to whispered promises passed down from ancient times: *"The Eternal has not forgotten. He will raise a deliverer. He will shatter these chains."*

The fields flourished. The clans expanded. And beneath the weight of their suffering, the people grew—not just in number, but in spirit. For oppression may harden hearts or break them, but in Velithar's case, it forged a nation ready to rise.

Two million souls. Six hundred thousand warriors. One people— awaiting the spark that would ignite their exodus and turn whispered hopes into roaring freedom. The Sacred Realms held their breath. The hour of reckoning drew near

The End of the Sojourn – Knowledge Amidst Chains.

Thus, the long sojourn of the Chosen People in the Realm of Zephyra drew to its close—a season marked by oppression and pain, yet not without purpose. Beneath the shadowed banners of Solkaris, where marble towers stretched toward the sun and the streets pulsed with merchants and mystics, the people of Velithar had been forged. Their bodies bore the scars of labor, yet their minds—sharpened in the crucible of hardship—gleamed with newfound knowledge.

Zephyra, for all its cruelty, was a land of wonders. Here, the architects harnessed stone and bronze to craft monuments that kissed the skies; here, healers brewed elixirs that seemed to dance with ancient alchemy; here, scribes etched knowledge onto scrolls spun from reed and silk, preserving wisdom older than many kingdoms. And the Velithari, though slaves in name, were not untouched by the currents of this civilization.

They labored in the vast gardens of Solkaris, where flora from distant realms thrived under enchanted irrigation systems. They hewed stone for temples adorned with intricate glyphs, learning the geometry and artistry that shaped the grand edifices. They served in the halls of scholars and healers, gleaning secrets of herbs that could mend wounds or still a racing heart. Traders of the Velithari people, permitted to barter for their meager sustenance, encountered maps that charted not only lands known but distant territories whispered of only in legend.

What began as survival became education. What was meant to break them instead became a forge of intellect and craft. Children born in Goshevar's valleys grew up hearing the ring of hammers in

Zephyra's forges, witnessing the delicate weavings of artisans, and tasting the complex languages of trade and diplomacy. Even the stars above seemed clearer from Zephyra's observatories, as if the Eternal had granted them glimpses of mysteries beyond mortal comprehension.

Yet for all they learned, the Velithari never forgot who they were. The stories of their forefathers—Zareon's journey, Eryon's sacrifice, Darion's lineage, Thalen's redemption—wove through their souls like threads of unbreakable silver. Knowledge was gained, yes, but identity was never lost.

By the time the countless moons had waxed and waned over their centuries-long stay, the people of Velithar emerged as more than a mere multitude of freed slaves. They carried with them the architectural wisdom of Zephyra, the healing arts gleaned from its apothecaries, the navigational skills learned from its merchants, and the agricultural innovations that had once yielded bounty even in famine. They were, by the will of the Eternal, shaped into a nation not only vast in number but rich in understanding.

But knowledge, for all its value, was not their ultimate inheritance.

Their true treasure was the promise passed down from generation to generation—that the Eternal had not abandoned them. That the Redeemer's line had not been extinguished. That the Covenant of Dawn still burned with unwavering light.

And so, as the book of their sojourn closed, another was about to be opened—one inked with fire and freedom, with miracles and judgments. The chains that once bound them would soon shatter. The land that awaited them stretched beyond the horizon, unseen but believed in, whispered of in every night's prayer.

The people of Velithar stood poised on the edge of destiny. Their backs to the alabaster towers of Zephyra, their faces turned toward the wilderness that beckoned. The Sacred Realms awaited the next chapter—a saga of deliverance, of covenant renewal, of a journey through fire into promise.

For though this book had ended, their story had only just begun.

Manufactured by Amazon.ca
Bolton, ON